WHEN THE LIGHT STILL SHONE

SAMANTHA GROSSER

SAM GROSSER
BOOKS

WHEN THE LIGHT STILL SHONE

ISBN: 978-0-6489635-8-5

Cover Design by ArtMishel

Chapter One

1995

It was cold at the graveside, a damp autumn day that held the promise of winter close behind. Now and then, rain splattered the mourners' faces as the breeze caught drops from the trees nearby. The vicar's voice ebbed and flowed with the wind but Georgia paid it no attention; her thoughts were with the man in the coffin in front of her.

Grandpa.

He had been more of a father than a grandfather, filling the void left by the man whose name her mother had never revealed. Even so, she was painfully aware she had barely known him, never glimpsing the man who existed behind the serious exterior. A slew of memories pattered through her thoughts – trips to the circus, the zoo, the cricket. Learning to drive and the gift of her first car. The proud smile when she won her school art prize. He had been kind and generous and, growing up, she had wanted for nothing. He had loved her, of that she had no doubt. But he had kept his true self a closely guarded secret that she suspected might be a legacy from the war, a detachment that allowed him to live alongside painful memories. As a girl, she had always hoped that when she got older he would share some of his experiences and let her inside the protective barrier: she had been eager to learn about his past, curious to know his thoughts and feelings on so many things. But she had never dared to ask, afraid to disturb his composure, and now it was too late.

She should have been braver, she thought, and asked him while she still had the chance.

Her fingers brushed against Nana's beside her, and the older woman turned briefly with a strained, sad smile. The usual glint was missing from her eyes, and Georgia could see only weariness and sorrow.

Had Nana known the truth of things? she wondered. Or had she, too, been held outside the walls her grandfather had built around himself? She simply couldn't imagine that they had ever exchanged whispered intimacies, secrets shared: her grandparents had always addressed each other with a quiet and respectful courtesy, and although it had been a peaceful house they had shared little laughter. Even when she went to live there as a child she had sensed an unspoken sadness in the air.

But still, she had loved him. Tears prickled behind her eyes. Whatever secrets he had treasured were safe forever now, and he was at peace.

On her other side she was aware of Scott, handsome in his dark suit, his muscled arm brushing hers now and then as she shifted her weight from foot to foot, toes growing numb in the cold. He stood quietly with his hands clasped together before him and his head bowed as though he were saying a prayer. But she knew him well enough to sense the boredom and impatience beneath the stillness, and she wished she hadn't asked him to come. She wondered now why she had, but she couldn't quite recall – in the days after the news of Grandpa's death she had not been thinking clearly. Perhaps she had hoped that in her grief Scott would show his softer side, rekindling the dwindling connection between them. Letting out a silent sigh, she thought she should have known better: she wasn't even sure any more he had a softer side.

The vicar's voice dwindled into silence as the burial service wound to a close and the coffin was lowered into the ground. Nana sniffed but she was upright and dry-eyed, and as they wandered across the cemetery towards the little hall for the wake, Georgia took her arm.

'Are you all right, Nana?'

'I'm fine, my dear.' The older woman patted Georgia's arm. 'I'm just glad it's over.'

Georgia nodded her agreement and flicked a glance back towards Scott who was following close behind, hands tucked in his trouser pockets, eyes scanning the horizon. Nana caught the movement from the side of her eye.

'You don't have to stay,' she said. 'I won't be offended.' She gave her granddaughter a smile that contained all the under-standing in the world and Georgia smiled in return, squeezing her grandmother's arm in gratitude.

'But I want to stay,' she replied.

They reached the little hall that stood beside the vicarage with its memories of childhood fetes and jumble sales, birthday parties and girl guide meetings. A buffet lunch had been laid out with tea and coffee cups at the ready, a pile of plates at one end of the table. Sandwiches and sausage rolls, cakes and fruit. The caterer slid discreetly out of sight towards the kitchen as the mourners filed in, and Georgia watched him go. After a moment, Scott broke away from them towards the food without a word, and the two women exchanged a look as he began to pile his plate from the platters of fruit.

Nana said, 'Are you happy with Scott?'

Surprised by Nana's question, Georgia observed him for a moment, running her eyes across the man who had been her partner since her last year at school, and turning over the answer in her thoughts. They'd been together so long she had never thought to question it – it had never crossed her mind that they could be apart.

Was she still happy with him?

She tilted her head and followed his movements as he stacked his plate with grapes and melon slices, taking in the easy confidence of his movements, and conscious of the well-honed muscles under the expensive suit, his strength and athleticism. Scott was a catch by any standards – handsome, charismatic, successful – and for a long time she had enjoyed every moment they had spent together. He had encouraged her to be adventurous; they had travelled and hiked, sky-dived and sailed, and she had liked who she was because of him.

But now that Nana had mentioned it, she had to admit she was starting to feel that something might be missing, an ache that pulled at her inside and cast a shadow across their life together. Beneath the taste for adventure, she realised, there was not much else they had in common. And now that her biological clock was starting to tick – friends getting married, having children – it had begun to matter that he showed no interest in settling down or having a family, that he never even mentioned a future together beyond choosing their next holiday.

She lowered her eyes away from her study of him and turned to her grandmother.

'I don't know any more,' she murmured.

'We'll talk later,' Nana whispered. Then, with a brief touch of her hand to Georgia's arm, she moved away as the first of the other mourners came to speak to her.

Standing alone, Georgia half watched the guests as they milled and talked and helped themselves to sandwiches and cake. Briefly, she remembered that she hadn't eaten but she made no move towards the spread, her guts tight and still churning. The caterer approached her with a concerned expression on his face.

'Is everything okay?' he asked.

He was a man about her own age with clear green eyes and neat open features, and he was observing her intently, waiting for her answer. She stared at him. She was at her grandfather's funeral – what did he expect her say? Then she realised he was talking about the food, and gave him an embarrassed smile.

'Yes,' she managed to say. 'Everything's fine. I'm just not hungry. It's been a difficult day.'

'Of course. I understand.' He returned her smile with an easy one of his own, then held out his hand.

'Ben Turner,' he said.

She took his hand, which was warm and dry, and introduced herself. Then they stood for a moment as they surveyed the scene before them, but the silence was comfortable and she felt no need to say anything more. After a minute, he turned to her again.

'Better get back to work. Nice to have met you.'

'You too,' she said.

He moved away towards the table and began to tidy up, rearranging the plates and collecting the dirties. Georgia drifted towards the window and gazed out across the graves beyond the glass. The sky had darkened, threatening more rain, but for now a pocket of sun glinted through a gap between the clouds and was shedding a golden light across the expanse of the cemetery lawn. It was quite beautiful – a tranquillity she had forgotten in the hurly-burly of her London life – and she sighed with an unexpected sweep of longing to return here that took her by surprise. Time was, she couldn't wait to leave the sleepy town for the bright lights of the city, and once she had finally made it to London, visits home had been rare and fleeting. But now the peace of it was surprisingly welcome. She really did want to stay for a while, she decided, and spend some time with her beloved nana, who was grieving.

Scott appeared at her shoulder and she wheeled towards him, startled out of her reverie.

'We should probably get going soon,' he said. 'It's a long drive home.'

She hesitated a moment before she replied. It wasn't often she didn't fall in with his plans; he was a hard man to say no to. She took a deep breath.

'I'm going to stay on for a few days,' she said, and gave him an apologetic smile that was not quite genuine. 'To be with Nana.'

He slid a glance towards the older woman, who was talking now to the vicar. 'She'll be fine,' he said. 'She's got lots of support here.'

'I want to stay,' she persisted, though she couldn't have said exactly why. 'Not just for Nana. He … Grandpa … was a father to me.'

Irritation flickered briefly across Scott's eyes, shadows in their depths.

'How will you get back?'

She shrugged. 'Train, probably. It's not impossible.'

He sighed. 'And work?'

'I'll call them. I'm owed some time. They can manage.' A dull office job in an insurance company where she was no more than a cog in a well-oiled machine. If she never went back there again, she wouldn't spare it another thought. And, she thought, with a barely suppressed sigh of her own, she doubted the company would even notice she was gone.

Taken aback by this unexpected act of independence, Scott regarded her for a moment as if appraising her anew; resenting the scrutiny, Georgia turned her face away to look over the hall at the scattered guests talking quietly in little groups, plates balanced awkwardly on upturned palms. There were people here she hadn't seen for far too long, people who had once made up her whole world: a couple of old school friends, a teacher, the doctor who had treated all her childhood ailments. He was grey-haired and retired now, but he still had the same kindly smile. She was pleased to see so many people had come, that Grandpa would be much missed in the community.

She brought her gaze back to Scott.

'I'll ring you when I'm coming back,' she said, with a defiant tilt of her chin.

He nodded. Then, with a cursory kiss to her cheek, he said goodbye and left.

. . .

Later, at Nana's house in Royal Lane, they sat at the kitchen table eating toast with honey and drinking tea. It had always been their special treat. Neither had eaten a bite at the wake.

'Scott didn't mind you staying?'

'I didn't give him a choice.'

Nana laughed and her whole face lit up. She was still lovely, Georgia thought, with sparkling eyes and silver hair that fell in neat and pretty curls around her temples. She laughed often, finding joy in the little things in her life and, not for the first time, Georgia wondered why she had married Grandpa, who was such a quiet and serious man: they had never seemed well-suited to each other. But then she thought of her relationship with Scott and, with an abrupt flash of insight, realised Nana probably thought the same about them. Were they well suited? She supposed they had been, once upon a time, but not, she thought sadly, any more.

She let her mind wander across the various couples she knew in her life, friends mostly – living together, getting engaged or married, starting a family. They all seemed happy enough, though it was hard to judge if they were good for each other. Did most people ever find their perfect partner, she wondered, or did they make do instead with the person they had ended up with, staying together out of habit and convenience, the very human urge not to be alone.

'How did you and Grandpa meet?' she asked, with sudden curiosity.

Now that he was gone, she wanted to know more and fill the empty space he had left behind him with a better understanding of the man he had been.

She knew only they had married after the war. She had always assumed they were sweethearts from a young age, but she knew very little of their history. They had rarely spoken about the past, lightly brushing off any questions, and in her fear of awakening unwelcome memories she had never ventured to ask any further. But now, given the closeness of Nana's questions about her relationship with Scott, she felt a little lift of hope that Nana might tell her more in return.

Her grandmother slid her gaze towards the kitchen window and regarded the coming drizzle and the grey afternoon with a wistful look. Georgia's own gaze followed. In the garden beyond, the apple trees were drooping in the damp, and the last of the autumn leaves were shiny with moisture. When her grandmother made no reply, she thought that perhaps she shouldn't have asked. Perhaps she should have waited for another day. But after a moment Nana turned her head away from the window with a half-suppressed sigh and replaced her cup carefully on its saucer.

'Were you childhood sweethearts?' Georgia prompted.

'No, not at all!' She shook her head. 'Although we did know each other slightly before the war...' She tilted her head and hesitated, as if reluctant to continue.

'Nana?'

Her grandmother let out a small sigh, as if resigning herself to tell a tale she would have preferred to forget. Georgia felt a small twinge of guilt for asking, and shrugged it away.

'Your grandfather was a local boy, and so we knew each other, growing up. After all, Sutton Heath is a very small town,' Nana went on after a moment. 'It was even smaller back then, no more than a village really, and everyone knew absolutely everyone. I grew up in the pub, remember, and it was the heart of the community. So I suppose we grew up together in a way.'

Georgia waited, barely breathing, afraid to interrupt in case Nana decided not to tell the story after all.

Nana took another mouthful of tea and looked at Georgia over the rim of her cup. 'You don't want to know all this. It's ancient history.'

'I *do* want to know.' Georgia was emphatic. 'Absolutely I do.'

Nana fingered the handle of her cup, turning it slowly back and forth on the saucer, watching the movement with unfocused eyes before she raised her head to stare out of the window once more, into the darkening garden beyond. The apple tree's dark branches were still just visible in the gloom, and the last glimmer of the day rimmed the clouds behind them.

'It looks like it's going to rain again,' she said, without turning.

Georgia said nothing, almost holding her breath with fear that her grandmother had said all she was going to say. Aware there was quite a story waiting to unfold, she gave Nana another gentle prompt.

'Nana?'

At the sound of her granddaughter's voice, Nana seemed to snap back into the moment. She wheeled to face her.

'I'm tired,' she said, with an unaccustomed brusqueness. 'It's been a big day. I'm going to have a bath and an early night. Will you be all right?'

'Of course,' Georgia answered, hiding her disappointment with what she hoped was a reassuring smile.

'Good night, then. I'll see you in the morning. Sleep well.'

She bent to give her a kiss on the cheek, her lips soft and warm, then turned and walked back across the kitchen to disappear into the hall.

Watching her go, Georgia was suddenly painfully aware of her frailty, but the air of sadness she carried with her seemed shadowed by something more complicated than her grief for Grandpa. She had seen the same sense of sorrow before today, Georgia realised, a brief light in her grandmother's face she had glimpsed now and then, just a flicker that was quickly hidden.

Taking the cups to the sink, Georgia rinsed them out, and when she raised her head to look out of the window above it, the glass showed only the kitchen's reflection, the garden beyond it lost in the darkness. Then she sat at the kitchen table again for a while, half listening to the sounds of Nana's footsteps passing to and fro upstairs, and the whirr of the water in the pipes as she ran the bath.

She loved this house where she had come to live after her mother's death, and she knew every creak and rattle, every corner. In summer, the rooms were bright and airy with large Victorian windows that opened onto a spacious garden; in winter, with the heavy curtains drawn, it was cosy against the night. Her eagerness to leave it behind all those years ago seemed absurd to her now, but she supposed the excitement of the city had been an irresistible lure, a desire for things new and unknown. And since then, she had barely ever looked back.

But now, as she looked around the kitchen with its old-fashioned dresser and the large table that had always been at the centre of the family, she gave herself a small smile, conscious that it felt far more like home than the luxury flat she shared with Scott in the beating heart of London. Perhaps she had needed to leave in order to appreciate how rare and precious its beauty really was, she reflected, because she realised now with a sudden acute awareness that the years she had spent in London had utterly failed to fill the need inside her. The city's charms were ephemeral and fleeting, and she had never truly felt that she belonged. It was Scott's world, not hers, and her soul still craved for something more, something of her own – though what it was she wanted exactly she could not have said.

Eventually, she heard the latch of her grandmother's bedroom door click into place for the final time and silence fell, the heavy and absolute quiet of the countryside. She tilted her head to listen but there was nothing. In London there was always noise – traffic, sirens, people, construction, the hum of a city that never ceased – and until just a few days ago she had welcomed it, taking it as a sign that she was making something of her life, an exciting world to inhabit. But here in Sutton Heath, wrapped in a beguiling tranquillity she thought she had forgotten, she let her thoughts drift back across the day, and wondered if she would ever hear the story that Nana had been so reluctant to tell.

Chapter Two

1995

In the morning Georgia came down to breakfast from a night of restless sleep to find the kitchen table strewn with old letters and photographs she had never seen before. A half-empty shoe box stood at one end with its lid thrown aside, and Nana was sifting through the contents. Utterly absorbed, she jumped in startlement when Georgia appeared in her line of sight. But when she raised her eyes they were bright with interest, a little of their old spark returning, and Georgia was delighted by the change. Nursing Grandpa through the weeks and months of his illness had taken its toll on her own health, her skin growing pale, dark shadows appearing beneath her eyes as the usual glimmer of mischief began to fade, so it was wonderful to see a little of her old self rekindling.

'What is all this?' Georgia asked, touching fingers to the corner of a photograph and swivelling it towards her. She ran her eyes across the picture and saw a black and white image of a group of airmen, seated on the grass before an airplane. They were laughing and one of them she saw now, had a small dog in his lap that was gazing happily at the camera, ears pricked and tongue lolling.

'You asked about the past,' Nana said, turning the photograph back towards her with a lowered glance across the image. 'Well, here it is.'

She made a spreading gesture with her hands, and Georgia noticed at once that she was no longer wearing the impressive diamond that had sat beside her wedding band for as long as she could remember. Instead, a simple ruby glinted with the morning sun, deep wine red and beautiful.

Georgia stared, speechless for a moment. Then, finding her voice at last, she managed to say, 'I don't understand.'

Her grandmother inclined her head, her lips just parting in a smile.

'Yes. It's complicated. Quite a story, in fact.'

Picking up a photograph from the table, she tilted it towards the light to see it more clearly. Georgia moved to stand at Nana's shoulder and looked at it too. The figures in the picture were hard to make out: the sepia image had faded across the intervening years and the couple's features were hard to distinguish. But it was clear enough that she could see they were two people very much in love – their faces were close, foreheads touching, and their eyes sparkled bright with happiness. Nana handed the photograph to Georgia and she took it nearer to the window to study it more closely, an unexpected quiver in her blood she couldn't quite explain. After a moment she turned back towards the table.

'Is this you?'

Nana nodded and raised her eyebrows.

'But the man ... that's not Grandpa, is it?'

'No. That's your real grandad. The love of my life.'

Georgia blinked in shock, and her lips moved as though she had something to say, but she could find no words at all.

'But ...' was all she could manage to stutter.

'I told you it was complicated.' Nana got up from the table and went to the counter to put on the kettle.

Georgia watched her, the still-lithe figure moving easily, dainty hands flitting above the teapot and cups as she prepared the tea. She said nothing, thoughts roiling with this startling piece of news as she lowered her gaze to examine the photograph again, running her eyes across the image of the two young people, happy and so obviously in love. After a moment, Nana turned and leaned her hips against the bench as the kettle hissed behind her.

'His name was Zack,' Nana said. 'Zachary Eldon, and he was an airman based at Little Sutton during the war.' She kept her voice carefully even, Georgia noticed, no betrayal of the emotion behind the words.

'What happened to him?' she asked, gently, certain of the answer even as she asked the question.

'He was shot down somewhere in Europe. That's all I know.'

Georgia said nothing, still trying to take in all that Nana had said, her whole past swept away into something new by this revelation. The kettle huffed to a boil and switched itself off and Nana turned away to make the tea. Georgia's gaze swept across the table as though all the photographs and letters before her could make the story clear in her head. When she looked up again, Nana was staring into the distance at some unknown thing, remembering. She began to speak again in so soft a voice that Georgia had to step closer to hear her.

'He went out with a different crew that day,' she murmured. 'On a different airplane, as a last-minute substitute. I didn't even know he was flying. It happened sometimes when a regular member of a crew got sick or injured. But they all hated doing it. The crews were very tight knit and they'd learned to trust each other. None of them ever wanted to fly with anyone else.' She stopped and took a deep breath, eyes once again sweeping the spread of telegrams and photographs and letters that were fanned across the table.

Georgia waited, conscious of her grandmother's hesitation and the sorrow in the recollection. Briefly, she wondered if the memories would prove too painful to share any more. But after a moment, Nana lifted her gaze from the table and gave a small, sad smile.

'I heard the news from his great friend, Freddie,' she said. 'He was one of the other gunners in Zack's usual crew. Their plane had been grounded for repairs ... the landing gear or something ... I can't remember. There's a photo of him in there somewhere – one of the crew had a Kodak, so there were always photos.' She waved her hand towards the table and made a small movement as if she were going to look for it but then stopped, eyes returning to gaze once more into the distance. 'I lost touch with him afterwards. He must have been shot down too, I suppose. Otherwise he would have visited. I was very fond of him.' She looked up, eyes bright with an intensity that Georgia had never seen in them before. 'The attrition rate was horrific – so many men who never came back. But they kept flying. Day after day after day.

Georgia found her voice at last. 'So all these years later you still don't know what happened to him?'

Nana shook her head. 'It was war, and it was enough to know I'd lost him.'

'Aren't you curious though?'

'Oh, I've sometimes wondered over the years – imagining all the different ways a man might die in a plane. I used to have nightmares about it.'

For a moment Georgia was silent, her thoughts curling around this unexpected glimpse into the past. Her real grandfather, and a secret all these years. Her own need to discover the truth burned inside her, a heat that travelled from her core to her fingertips. Why had no one ever told her? Why had his very existence been denied?

She thought of Grandpa, buried only yesterday, and a twinge of sorrow turned in her gut. Had he known? She drew in a deep breath to quell the rising tide of feeling.

'I could look into it if you like and do some research?' she murmured. 'I'm sure there would be records somewhere. I know I'd love to know.'

Nana hesitated, and Georgia understood that long-buried feelings were beginning to stir, memories she had set aside all through the long and loveless years of her marriage to Grandpa. She could see the indecision in the quick darting movements of Nana's eyes, hope and fear of disappointment both vying to be heard, a wound about to be reopened.

'It's worth a try, isn't it?' she prompted, when the silence began to grow long. 'To find out what really happened to him?'

Her grandmother drew in a long deep breath, as though she were steeling herself for some ordeal. Perhaps she was.

'I don't know,' she said again, lowering her head away, indecision written clear in the fretful darting of her gaze across the floor. 'I don't know if I want to disturb all that sorrow again. It's in the past, long buried.'

Georgia scanned the scattered photographs.

'But you haven't forgotten,' she said gently. Then, 'Did he give you that ring? It's beautiful.'

At the counter, Nana let out a long low sigh as her right hand seemed to reach of its own accord to touch the left, turning the ruby lightly on her finger. There was a long silence. Outside, the postman's van drew up in the lane and they heard his footsteps crunching on the gravel path, the light thud of the post landing on the mat behind the door. Neither of them moved.

'Yes,' Nana whispered at last. 'It was my engagement ring. We bought it in London …' She trailed off, eyes clouding over. Then, with a visible effort – a deep inhale and shoulders straightening – she raised her head and met Georgia's gaze.

'Perhaps you're right. Perhaps it would be good to know after all this time, and lay those ghosts to rest.'

She gave a small tight smile that belied the effort Georgia knew it must have cost her, and turned once more to finish making the tea.

They spent all morning sifting through the photographs, old letters Nana had received from friends, hasty notes that Zack had scrawled, ancient paperwork. They found Georgia's mother's birth certificate, and Nana recounted all she could remember of Zack's past from before they had met.

The small town in Idaho that he came from.

'Bliss, it was called,' she said, 'I always remember that – such a lovely name for a place.'

His younger sister Louise, who had not long left home to work in a munitions factory.

His drunken father.

The crew of the *American Maiden*, and the men who had been his friends.

Georgia listened intently, and though she had a hundred questions she wanted to ask, she let her grandmother tell the story in her own way. Then, when Nana finally paused in her recollection, and raised her eyes again to the window as if looking back into years long past, she turned to her grandmother with a hesitant question.

'Did Grandpa know about all of this?'

The question seemed to catch the older woman off-guard. Lowering her gaze away from the window she hauled her thoughts back to the morning in front of her. She let out a half-laugh, half-sigh before she could gather her thoughts to answer.

'He knew,' she murmured. 'Of course he knew. I was an unmarried woman with a young child, and it was common knowledge in the village that Zack had been the father. But we never spoke of it. You see, your grandpa had never made it into uniform, and though as an engineer his work was desperately important, he never quite got over the shame that he hadn't had the chance to fight for his country. He already felt Zack's presence looming large: an airman who had made the ultimate sacrifice, the true father of our child. He never said as much of course, but I could tell.'

Georgia waited, hoping for more, but whatever Nana had been going to say, she had changed her mind before the words reached her lips.

'But what about Mum?' Georgia asked. 'If Zack was her

real father, then she wasn't Grandpa's true daughter. That must have been difficult.' She spoke gently, understanding her questions were opening the way to painful memories.

'Ah, yes. Well, your mum's existence couldn't be denied, of course, and I was adamant she should know who her real father was. His name was on her birth certificate after all. We had some terrible arguments about it at the time and for what it was worth, I got my way. But the times were different then. People wanted to forget about the war and put it all behind them. They were looking towards the future, not the past. I told your mum about Zack when she was a girl but she just wasn't interested. Grandpa was her dad in all the ways that mattered, and she wanted to be like her friends. She didn't want to have a complicated story in her background.'

'She never told me.'

'You were very young when she passed away. Perhaps she would have told you in time.'

Georgia nodded, unconvinced. She had never known her own father, her past on that side utterly unknown too. A sliver of anger at the secrets that her mother had kept from her crept around her heart, and she had to clamp her jaw against the rising tide of emotions.

Nana must have sensed the storm inside her and guessed the reasons for it, because she said then, 'Your mother was a good person. She was kind and funny and full of love. But she fell in with the wrong crowd for a while, and spent time with men who weren't good to her. She was convinced it was better for you never to know your father. She had her reasons – she was trying to protect you.'

Georgia swallowed down the swell of tears in her throat. 'She told you that?'

'Not in so many words, but I could read between the lines.'

She let this new knowledge percolate through her thoughts. She had always imagined her father had simply upped and left when he found out there was going to be a child, leaving her mother with a broken heart. She had never suspected her mother might have chosen to hide her away for her own protection. Another layer of the story seemed to peel away, and she mourned again for all the years she had spent without her.

'You lost the love of your life and then your daughter,' she said. 'That must have been terrible.'

'Yes,' Nana agreed, blinking. 'But I had you, and you were a gift. Looking after you kept me together when everything else seemed to fall apart. You brought the light back into my life.'

They embraced, and Georgia blinked back her own tears.

Then, drawing away, she said, 'Tell me how you and Zack met. Tell me everything. I want to know it all.'

Chapter Three

1943

Saturday night, and the bar of the Queen's Head was crowded, the hubbub of voices skirling off the walls so loud it was difficult to think. Tension simmered, the resentment of the locals against the airmen from the newly built base in their crisp, smart uniforms, matched by the Americans' contempt for those men who were not serving. Peggy touched a hand to her temple in recognition of the headache that was starting to form, then wove easily between the tables to collect the empty glasses. An RAF officer sitting near the door caught her eye and smiled before draining his pint and getting up to leave.

Her father was watching with eagle eyes from behind the bar where he was polishing a glass, and the drinkers mostly treated her respectfully, at least to her face. David Ellis was a strongly built man, and there was a photograph on the pub wall of him in his youth wearing boxing gloves, arms raised in triumph. Returning to the bar, Peggy set down the tray next to her father, and he lifted his eyebrows with a smile of question.

'What do you think?' he murmured, and made a small

gesture of his head that encompassed the rowdy crowd. She knew straight away what he meant.

On the other side of the room, a trio of locals were sliding hostile glances towards the airmen, who were recounting tales of bravado with increasing volume, hooting in appreciation and stamping their feet on the floorboards.

'I think there's going to be trouble soon,' she replied, and she had to shout to make herself heard as she set the glasses on the draining board under the bar, ready to wash.

From somewhere out of their sight, there came the sudden shatter of a glass being smashed. The noise sliced through the tension, vibrating like a violin string wound too tight and about to snap. Flinching at the sound, she darted a look towards the direction of the crash. Howls of laughter rose from the American end of the room, filling the bar.

'Play something,' her father suggested, nodding towards the old piano against the wall, 'while I clean that up.'

Peggy sighed. She hated playing in the bar on nights like this, battling against the noise and disquiet, struggling to make herself heard. But she knew it might help dissipate the tension – sometimes the music seemed to work the magic of a snake charmer that beguiles the serpent and renders it harmless. Music could draw the men out of their violent mood, providing a distraction that reminded them of other times, other places.

Stripping off her apron, she wound between the tables and drinkers to the piano and settled herself on the stool. Then, taking a moment to straighten her skirt and flick back a stray strand of hair from her face, she opened the lid. She had played this piano ever since she could remember and though she was no virtuoso, she loved its worn keys and the way that at times it offered an escape from her troubles.

Now though, as her fingers rested on the keys, she had to fight to compose herself, pulses quick, nerves rattling through her limbs. Behind her, she was conscious of the roar of men's voices and the undertones of tension. She turned briefly to survey the crowd at her back and caught her father's eye. He nodded and gave her an encouraging smile.

With a deep breath, she lowered her fingers to the keyboard and played a chord that breathed through the pub. Had anyone noticed? She doubted it. She played another, and the clamour all around seemed to dim a notch. Raising her eyes, she searched the prints on the wall above the piano for inspiration. A framed painting of a storm at sea that she had always liked hung above the piano, and so she picked out the first few bars of "Stormy Weather," gently, warming up her fingers, testing. She hadn't played in a while. But the music was familiar and soothing, a song she loved, and her nerves quickly ebbed away, leaving only a barely noticed residue to shadow the pleasure of it.

The voices closest to the piano, mostly locals, dwindled, and she was aware of their growing attention as they waited for her to sing. The hush rippled across the bar and even the airmen at the far end seemed to quieten down. But their voices had already retreated to the edges of her thoughts – she was absorbed by the effort of the music, focused on remembering the notes, steeling herself to sing.

When she began the song at last, there was no trace left of her nerves. Her voice was true and clear, carrying sweetly across the bar so that the last of the rowdiness was finally hushed. The locals exchanged smiles of pleasure – this girl they had known all her life making them proud – and the airmen shared glances of surprise.

She finished the song and the pub erupted in cheers and whistles. Peggy looked for her father across the throng and he met her gaze with a smile of satisfaction.

'Keep going,' he mouthed. 'Sing something else.'

She nodded and bent over the piano once more, pausing for a moment as she considered what to play next, fingers resting idly on the keyboard, still undecided. Then one of the airmen slid on to the stool beside her and she looked up at him, startled. She hadn't heard him approach. But his head was lowered, his long fingers already testing the keys, and when he started to play he teased a sound from the old piano she had never suspected was possible – sweet and mellow tones that spoke of another life a world away. His hands slid easily over the keys, mesmerising to watch, and when she raised her head to look at him again, he met her gaze this time with a smile. Moss-coloured eyes, she noticed, beneath a broad forehead, and full lips with straight white teeth. Eyes that held hers now with uncomfortable intensity, so that she was abruptly aware of their closeness on the stool, thighs touching.

'Do you mind if I play along?' he asked then, softly, kindly, and she laughed, disconcerted.

'No, of course not,' she managed to say.

He nodded his thanks and turned his attention once more to the music. She waited, entranced by the movements of his hands as he picked out passages of unfamiliar melodies, slipping deftly from one into the next, until at last she recognised the song.

He lifted his head and looked at her again, as the first few notes of "As Time Goes By" began to fill the air.

'You know this one?'

It was her turn to nod and, though she didn't know it well, she began to sing softly along, faltering her way through the words. After a moment, the airman joined her, harmonising perfectly, and the last dregs of conversation fell to silence as the music cast its spell across the pub. It was a beautiful song from a beautiful movie. She had gone with her friend Sylvia to see *Casablanca* in town a couple of months before and the melody had seemed to her to contain all the sorrow of the war, and all the love that could never be because of it. Unfamiliar emotions welled inside her as she sang and played alongside the airman, whose eyes contained a smile she hoped was meant only for her.

When the song ended, there was a moment of silence before the applause began and the two of them looked at each other, surprised and delighted by their unexpected connection. Before now, she had shared the general belief that the airmen were rough and uncultured, arrogant and rowdy. Like most of the locals, she had viewed them *en masse* – the American invasion – barely noticing the individual men behind the group façade. They seemed to travel in packs and if she had seen them at all, they had been as men from another world, foreign and unknowable. For the first time, it crossed her mind that the airmen might see British people the same way.

He tilted his head and smiled, and with the movement his whole face lit up, green eyes sparkling. She was aware of her cheeks flushing red, but whether the feeling came from the pleasure in the music or the thrill of his attention, she could not have said. She smiled in return.

'Shall we play something else?' he asked, and even as she nodded, his fingertips were already stroking the keys, picking out the first few notes of a Bing Crosby song she took a moment to identify as "Moonlight Becomes You". But before she could open her mouth to sing, a man's form loomed into view close to the American, his shadow falling across the keyboard. Her head jerked up in alarm. The airman seemed to pay him no attention, eyes still lowered to watch his hands as they danced across the keys. But she was aware of the sudden tension in his body close beside her, the muscles in his thighs next to hers braced and ready.

'Are you flirting with my girl?' the man demanded. He placed a hand on the American's shoulder and his face was red and contorted with rage.

'Terry!' Peggy spat his name with fury. She was not his girl. She was nobody's girl but her own. She swung off the stool and stood up, finding herself at the airman's back as she faced her old friend.

The airman let out a slow breath and his hands slowed to a halt on the keyboard. The silence hung in the air, and all eyes in the pub were trained on them as if they were lit by a spotlight.

'I'm not flirting with anyone,' the American said. 'I'm just making music.'

Terry's hands balled and unballed into fists at his side, and in his dark eyes flashed a light she realised, with a lurch of anger in her gut, was jealousy.

'Well, find someone else to make music with,' the Englishman snarled.

The airman straightened slightly then turned to Peggy at his back. 'Are you his girl?'

27

She shook her head, and he looked up at Terry with a shrug, still standing over him. Panic thrilled through her limbs in anticipation of the fight she knew was coming, and she tried to find her father across the sea of heads. But for once he was nowhere to be seen and she held her breath as the airman slowly got to his feet.

In the silence, an American voice she could not pinpoint rang loud across the pub.

'Hey, mister! Why aren't you in uniform?'

'None of your bloody business,' Terry roared, searching for the man who had spoken, and in the moment of his distraction the airman took his chance and shoved him hard in the chest, so that he stumbled backwards and almost fell.

Instinctively, Peggy touched her fingers to the American's arm, hoping to stop him.

'Please don't,' she whispered, and though he brushed her hand lightly with his own, he was already moving forward to meet Terry, who had recovered his feet and was after blood.

Before the two men had struck the first blow the whole pub exploded into battle, the long-simmering tensions finding release at last. Peggy closed the lid of the piano and stood at its side, watching helpless as the brawl gained momentum, chairs and tables swinging, glasses crashing and shattering. The musician had beaten Terry into submission and the Englishman was cowering now in the corner, nursing his face with one hand as the other man turned away. For two breaths she watched him, supposing he was searching out his next victim, but when his eyes lighted on her he stepped forward and reached for her hand.

'Let's go,' he said.

She cast a wild gaze across the pub, still hoping to find her father, but in the hurly-burly she could not see him. Somewhere, far away, the faint wail of a siren pierced the night. Her father must have called the police at the first sign of violence. She grabbed his hand.

'Come on,' she said. 'This way.'

She led him out the back way through the kitchens where she spent most of her days preparing food for the pub, and along the narrow corridor that led to the yard behind the building. Outside, it was a warm summer night, the very last glow of the twilight still clinging to the edges. A layer of high cloud scudded on the breeze and a bright half-moon lit the courtyard, so that they could see each other quite clearly despite the lateness of the hour.

They stopped, breathing hard, and it took her a few breaths to realise that her hand was still in his. She looked at it, self-conscious and unsure, before she carefully drew it away. Then they stood in awkward silence, and the din of the brawl inside was muffled so that it seemed like something that was happening in another place altogether and nothing to do with them. She was only vaguely aware of the approaching sirens.

'I should probably go,' he said at last. 'I don't want to be here when the MPs arrive.'

'You can cut across the field at the back.' She gestured with her hand. 'That way you can avoid the road.'

His eyes followed the direction of her hand. 'Can you show me?'

She hesitated. 'I shouldn't,' she said. 'I mean, I don't even know your name.'

'Yeah, that's true.' He tilted his head in agreement. 'But we've sung "As Time Goes By" together, so that's gotta count for something. Doesn't that make us ...' He trailed off with a shrug.

'Partners?' she offered, and, after a moment's consideration, he nodded.

'Yeah. I like that. Partners.'

The sirens were close now, screaming through the night, and he needed to be gone. But he waited, still hoping, she supposed, for her company on the long walk back to the airbase.

'So if I tell you my name will you show me the way?'

In spite of all she had been told her whole life about finding herself alone with a man she didn't know, she couldn't help but laugh. She wanted to stay with him, to be in the light of his smile a little longer, and the instinct in her gut was to trust him. Besides, she had no desire to go back into the pub where she knew there would be bloody noses and a mess to clear up. Local police and military policemen asking questions. It could wait, she decided, and she would see to it when all the brawlers had been taken away.

She lifted her head to meet the question in his eyes and felt the same flush of pleasure across her cheeks as before.

'Yes,' she replied. 'If you tell me your name, I'll show you the way.'

Chapter Four

1943

His name was Zack Eldon, he told her, and he was a tail-gunner in a B17 known as the *American Maiden.*

'I got here a couple of weeks ago,' he said.

'Have you flown much?' Peggy asked.

She found it difficult to imagine this quiet young man with his musical hands 25,000 feet above Europe in the heat of battle, facing flak and German fighter planes. Her heart seemed to tighten at the thought of it.

'No,' he replied. 'Not yet. Only in training. Our Bomb Group is brand new – they're still building the base, so we haven't started flying missions yet.'

She could think of nothing to say and so they walked in silence for a moment, side by side along the edge of the field, close to the bramble hedge where the first blackberries were just beginning to appear. She was aware of his warmth and life; skin and blood and sinew under the uniform. She had never been so aware of a person as a living being before and she had to fight the urge to take his hand in hers again. But the silence was comfortable – she was easy in his company, as though they had known each other always.

'Who's Terry?' Zack asked. He cradled one fist in his palm and rubbed his knuckles, so that she asked, 'Did you hurt yourself?'

'No,' he answered with a smile. 'I barely touched him. He's not much of a fighter – I'm not surprised he's not in uniform.'

'He's just qualified as a doctor,' she explained, defending him instinctively. 'We've been friends since we were children.'

'He seems to think you're more than friends.'

'We're not,' she insisted, slowing her steps a little and turning her head to look at him. He glanced her way and met her look with a nod of acknowledgement. 'Never have been. Never will be.'

But as she said the words she began to wonder how long Terry had wanted more, and how she had never realised it. It had never even crossed her mind to think of him that way. Had she unknowingly encouraged him? Had their friendship given him false hope? A small shudder of anxiety rippled through her.

'I didn't hurt him much,' Zack said, as though he had understood her worries. 'Just his pride, I reckon. He'll be fine.'

Reassured, she smiled, and they picked up their pace again.

Too soon, they came to the gate that led out to the lane. Zack vaulted it in one easy movement that made her laugh with surprise as she unhooked the latch and opened it to slide through the gap. Then they stood at the side of the road that led to the base, looking towards it though it was invisible now in the darkness. The road shone white with moonlight, and she looked up at him, aware again of his closeness, the warmth of life in his blood.

'You can find your way from here?' she said.

He nodded but did not turn away, prolonging the moment, and she was glad. She liked the way she felt with him. It was an excitement and a pleasure just to be in his company and as they stood there, reluctant to part, she half-toyed with the possibility of walking with him the whole way to the base. But she let the idea slip away as soon as she thought of it – she would be walking for most of the night, and she would have to return alone.

'Can I see you again?' Zack broke the silence. There was an unexpected uncertainty in his voice as if he were afraid she would refuse, and she felt herself falling a little bit deeper. Her breathing quickened in anticipation.

'I'd like that,' she whispered.

Somewhere high above them in the distance a lone engine interrupted the night, and Zack raised his head to search for the source of the sound. 'Sounds like one of yours, heading home,' he said.

She nodded her agreement. Then, with a touch of his hand to his temple in a salute of farewell, he turned and walked away.

Peggy stood and watched him go as his lean form dwindled into the night. Once, just before the dark swallowed him completely, he turned back and waved. She raised her arm in return, then slid back through the gate and hurried home.

'Oh, thank God!' Her father's relief to see her was written in his face. 'I didn't know where you'd got to.'

The bar was a mess. Bits of broken chairs and stools were littered across the stone floor, and underfoot crunched with broken glass. Her father was standing in the centre of it all with a broom in his hand, and Terry was perched on a barstool holding a compress to his cheek.

'I'm sorry, Dad,' she said, with an apologetic smile. 'I didn't mean to worry you. I was just keeping out of the way till it was over.'

'Don't lie,' Terry snapped. 'I saw you leave with that airman.'

Peggy stooped to pick up the broken leg of a stool before she answered, breathing deeply to quell the rising surge of anger. This was his fault, this destruction. He had been the catalyst that set the powder keg on fire.

'I showed him the way out, that's all,' she managed to reply, through lips clamped tight with her fury. 'Not that it's any of your business.'

Tossing the broken stool leg on to the pile, she reached to take the broom from her father and began to sweep while he righted the upturned tables, examining the chairs and stools for damage. With all the shortages of wartime they would be hard to replace, but perhaps he would be able to fix some of them: he was handy with tools – before he took over the pub he had worked on the land, where resourcefulness is a way of life.

'You could help,' Peggy shot at Terry, who was still seated at the bar, watching her as she worked.

'I'm injured,' he replied, with a hurt look on his face.

She recalled Zack's words – *I barely touched him* – and had to suppress a smile. Her father caught her eye across the bar and raised his eyebrows, and she smothered a laugh.

'It isn't funny.' Terry climbed down from the stool with exaggerated care. 'I'm going home.'

Neither Peggy nor her father wished him farewell, but Peggy followed him to the door to lock up behind him. As he stepped out into the night, still making a show of nursing his cheek with the compress, he turned back towards her.

'You want to be careful, Peggy Ellis,' he warned. 'Going with an American will only lead to trouble. You mark my words.' Then, before she had a chance to reply, he wheeled abruptly away and stalked off down the high street. 'You'll be sorry.' His parting shot echoed through the empty street.

She slid the bolts home on the door behind him, and weariness began to flood through her limbs as all the excitement of the evening drained out of her abruptly. She stood with her back against the wooden slats, surveying the wreckage, and her father looked up from the table he had just set upright.

'Are you all right, love?'

She nodded. 'I just wish Mum were here. I still can't believe she's gone.'

'I know,' he agreed.

But her mother had been killed early in the war, caught in a German air raid in Norwich where she had been doing volunteer work. The pain of the grief had yet to lose the sharpness of its cutting edge, and Peggy missed her each and every day.

'Did the police arrest many?' she asked, forcing her mind away from thoughts of her mother as she picked her way over the broken glass to retrieve the broom.

'Most of them got away,' her father replied. 'The airmen too. By the time the MPs arrived it was all but over.'

'I'm glad.'

For all the damage they had caused she couldn't bring

herself to wish them harm. The Americans were young men at war and the urge to violence simmered too close to the surface. They looked down on the local men who worked on the land, men who were classified as essential workers and not allowed to join up. Despite the nation's need for the food they produced, most of them chafed bitterly against the restriction, eager to do their bit and go to war. They felt their exclusion from the forces as a stain on their character, and they resented the presence of the airmen with their money and accents and smart tailored uniforms that offered British girls a glimpse of glamour. Add alcohol into the mix, and those resentments could be the spark that lit the tinder keg.

It was a pity, Peggy thought, as she swept up the splinters of wood and glass – they were all on the same side, after all.

She swept around the piano, crouching down to collect a shard of glass that lay underneath it, and an image of Zack trod again across her thoughts. With another flush of pleasure that warmed her cheeks, she recalled his closeness beside her on the piano stool, their voices raised in harmony, and his smile when she agreed to see him again. Idly now, barely paying any attention to her sweeping, she retraced the walk they had made together in her mind's eye, recalling every look and every word that had passed between them, the warmth of his body next to hers, and allowed herself to dream of seeing him again.

Chapter Five

1943

On Sundays the pub didn't open until midday, and in the morning Peggy went with her father to church. It was more from custom than conviction – her mother had been the one with faith, and it still seemed wrong that she was not there alongside them as they made their way through the village without her. But despite her lack of faith, Peggy loved the ancient medieval building with its squat square tower and grey flint walls, and the long centuries of history that pervaded it. She could almost sense the ghosts of all those generations of worshippers with their hopes and prayers and sorrows. Though the services bored rather than inspired her – the vicar preached an unforgiving creed – it was a chance to catch up with the rest of the villagers; in these uncertain times she found solace in the weekly gathering together of the community – a sense of belonging, hardships shared.

'He was talented, that airman last night. I haven't heard piano playing like that for a long time,' her father said with a quick turn of his head towards her as they walked together through the cool damp of the morning. High clouds shifted slowly overhead and a watery sun peered now and then around the edges, casting a golden glow across the village.

Peggy smiled, aware of the flush that crept across her cheeks at the thought of him. She lowered her head away, hoping her father wouldn't see.

'Yes,' she replied, keeping her voice as even as she could. 'He was.'

'And nice-looking too.'

Her father kept his eyes forward this time, but when she slid a look at him she could see the crinkle of a smile at the corners of his eyes, the edges of his mouth suppressing an upward curve.

She laughed then, unable to hold in the pleasure.

'He was lovely,' she agreed.

They reached the church. A small crowd of parishioners had gathered in the churchyard and, even from the road, they could tell the talk was all about the fight at the pub.

They exchanged a look. 'Just be careful, love,' her father said. 'I don't want you getting hurt.'

'I will, Dad,' she replied. 'Thank you.'

They stepped through the kissing gate and made their way along the winding path that led between the graves, skirting the little crowd, reluctant to get drawn into the gossip and conjecture. A voice called out to them as they passed but her father simply raised a hand in acknowledgement and kept on walking. Peggy kept her head down and followed him into the church. Inside, they took their usual seats halfway back along the aisle. Within, the conversation was more muted, and Peggy waved to her friend Sylvia on the other side of the church before she settled into place to wait for the service to begin.

Gradually the little church filled and the air vibrated with the usual hushed chatter as the congregation waited for the vicar to appear. Idly, to fill the time, Peggy let her gaze trail around the church, and when she chanced to glance behind her, her attention caught by a child's high wail, her eyes lighted on a couple of American servicemen standing right at the back of the nave, as though they were unsure of their welcome. Her heart lurched in her chest in the moment that she realised one of them was Zack, and it was all she could do to stop herself running along the aisle towards him. He was watching her, and when he caught her gaze at last, she saw her own pleasure reflected in his smile as he grinned at her.

Then the vicar arrived, young and earnest, his brow slick with sweat as he looked out from the lectern over his congregation. But when he began to speak she barely heard a word of what he said: all her thoughts were on the man at the back of the church, and her whole body seemed to throb with impatience for the service to end. She could feel the patter of her heartbeat, heat in her limbs.

Zack was not the first airman to worship at St Helen's – there had been others now and then in the months since the Americans had started to arrive. Though the airbase held its own services, she imagined that sometimes the men just wanted to explore the place to which the war had led them. A medieval church must be a strange and wonderful thing to an American, she thought, and realised how much she took that connection to the past for granted.

The service seemed to go on forever. Hymns and prayers and an interminable sermon on victory achieved through faith. Did the Germans preach the same thing? she found herself wondering. Did God listen? She supposed German mothers prayed for their sons the same as the British and Americans – so how did He possibly decide who to spare and who to take? It was far beyond her understanding, and as the congregation stood up to sing another hymn she let the thought trail away.

She sang without giving any consideration to the words, allowing the music to wash across her as a sea of sound, and despite the whole congregation of people all around her she was conscious only of Zack, straining to pick out his voice among the chorus. But although she could not hear him, she could sense the weight of his gaze on her back, and the impulse to turn to him was so compelling she had to brace her muscles against the temptation and force her head to face the front as the worshippers sat and stood and knelt, and the vicar seemed to drone on without end.

Finally, finally, the last prayers and blessing finished and she clambered to her feet, her heartbeat drumming quickly with excitement, eager for Zack's company. But as she turned to sidle along the row, she caught a glimpse of Terry further forward with his father. She wondered she hadn't noticed him before – he must have been there the whole service, she realised. But he was looking around the church now, as if searching for someone, and she quickly turned away so that their glances could not meet. She was still boiling inside at his claim on her at the pub, and the blame for the fight and the damage she laid squarely at his feet. Casting another glance towards the rear of the church, she saw that the airmen hadn't yet left, still standing awkwardly near the wall. Had Terry seen them yet? She didn't want to think about how he might react when he did.

Risking a quick look in his direction, she saw he was now

in conversation with the elderly woman beside him and so, with a murmured word to her father, she slipped along the row, hoping to escape before he could waylay her.

In the aisle, it seemed as though the whole village was milling and blocking her way, and by the time she had woven her way between them towards the door the airmen were nowhere to be seen. A sense close to panic blossomed in her chest that Zack would leave before she had the chance to speak to him. Surely he had come there to see her? Surely he would wait?

Outside, in the church porch, the vicar was exchanging words with the exiting parishioners and she had to squeeze through the little crowd that filled the small space.

'Excuse me, excuse me.'

The villagers stepped aside to let her pass and the vicar, catching the movement, lifted an uncertain hand as though to stay her. But she replied only with a quick apologetic smile in his direction and kept on her way. Then, finally past the huddle of people in conversation on the path, she stopped and looked out over the graveyard, eyes searching, until they lighted on the airmen a little distance away. They were wandering between the graves and reading the headstones. At the sight of them she let out a breath of relief: he had waited after all.

She took a moment to watch them, observing their easy friendship and the smiles and conversation they exchanged. Zack was very smart and handsome in his olive uniform and service cap, and as she remembered their hands close together on the piano keys, she felt the heat that rose across her neck and face again, flushing her skin. Then, as he raised his head to glance back towards the church, Zack saw her at last and a smile lit across his features. He straightened up and turned to face her.

Taking a deep breath that did nothing to calm her racing heart, Peggy picked her way across the unmown grass towards him. When she reached him she stopped, and they stood awkwardly for a moment: all the ease of the previous evening seemed to have left them and they were unsure how to be with each other.

After a moment, he gestured to the man beside him. 'This is my friend, Freddie,' he said. 'We're part of the same crew.'

She turned to the other man with a greeting and a smile and recognised his face from the crowd at the pub, fair and freckled with a mop of sandy hair.

'Nice to meet you,' Freddie said. Then, tactfully, he withdrew, feigning interest in a pair of headstones a little distance away.

'Do you have time to walk for a while?' Zack asked, and she nodded.

They turned from the church and headed out on to the road, strolling southwards away from the village towards the river. Even though the day was cool for the time of year it was a pleasant walk, and the day promised to be clear, offering glimpses of powder-blue sky between the sunlit clouds. Briefly, she wondered if Terry had noticed her leave and if he had seen she was with Zack, but the thought didn't trouble her for long.

At first they walked without talking, still searching for the lightness of the previous evening, and as the chatter from the churchyard dwindled into silence behind them, the only sound was the tread of their boots on the road. But even though they said nothing, she was comfortable beside him – it didn't seem to matter whether they spoke or not. Like being with an old friend, she thought, and gave herself a smile at the idea of it.

'What's funny?' He had caught the smile.

'Nothing, really,' she replied, suddenly self-conscious. Then, deciding that perhaps he would like to know, she said, 'Only that I like being with you even when there seems to be nothing to say. Like we've known each other for ages.'

'Old pals.'

'Exactly.'

They reached the river and stopped on the bank in the shade of the trees to watch the water for a while as it meandered away from the village, cool and deep. A pair of ducks paddled past them, heading downstream, and on the opposite shore a copse of pine trees broke the flatness of the fields beyond. It was one of her favourite places.

'I used to come here with my friend for picnics sometimes,' she said, 'when we were growing up.'

'It's beautiful.'

A quietness settled around them that was broken only by the soft gurgle of the water, and the intermittent coo-coo of a pigeon from somewhere out of sight.

'Where are you from?' she asked.

He gave an equivocal tilt of his head. 'From a small town in Idaho you've never heard of – and I left it as soon as I could.'

'Where did you go?'

'New York. I played piano in bars for a while, then the war came along and I joined up.'

Ah, she thought. 'That's why your playing is so good – you're a professional.' She smiled in admiration. 'Who taught you to play?'

'My Sunday school teacher. I used to go to her house after school to practise. It started as a way to avoid going home but in the end I went because I loved it.'

'Things were bad at home?'

He hesitated and his eyes tracked the flight of a crow high above the opposite bank, its black form clear against the grey bank of incoming cloud. She wondered if she should have asked. Then he lowered his gaze and turned to her.

'Yeah,' he said. 'It was bad. Dad drank a lot. He probably still does – it's been a long time since I last heard from him. I get the odd letter from my sister now and then but she's moved away now too. She's doing war work, in a factory somewhere.'

Peggy could think of nothing to say in reply and they wandered on, following the ducks downriver. Raising her head skyward, she saw that the bank of cloud had thickened, covering the sun. Without it, the morning turned chilly and she shivered.

'You're cold,' he said. 'Is there somewhere we can go?'

'Not really. It's Sunday and nothing's open. Let's just walk. I'll soon warm up.'

They set off along the riverbank, striding across the grass, and with the movement it didn't take long to get warm again. They began to talk more easily then, about all sorts of things – their families and childhoods, music they liked and the books they had read. Peggy wanted to hear more about Zack's life in New York: it seemed impossibly glamorous to her – a world away from her life in sleepy Sutton Heath, a place she could only dream of.

'After the war I'll take you there,' he said, and with his words they slowed their steps. They had come to a wooden bridge that spanned the narrow waterway and they made their way to the centre of it, leaning on the rail and looking down into the current as it swirled and eddied on its way towards the sea, bright and clear.

'Do you mean that?' She turned to him beside her. His arm brushed hers with the movement, and she remembered again the touch of his thigh against hers on the piano stool, their shoulders bumping as they played.

Zack took a moment to reply, his eyes still following the movement of the river for another breath, before he lifted his head to meet her question.

'Yes,' he said softly. 'I do.'

Her breathing seemed to stop in her chest.

'I'd like that,' she managed to whisper.

He nodded slightly as if they had made a deal, then lifted one hand to brush back a stray tendril of hair that had fallen across her face. The brush of his fingertips was exquisite, and she held her breath, not daring to move in case she spoiled the perfection of the moment as he trailed the backs of his fingers across her cheek and brought them to rest beneath her chin, tilting it upwards towards him.

He was very close to her. She could feel the warmth of his breathing and the lift and fall of his chest. Slowly, he lowered his head to hers, and their lips met, briefly, gently, no more than the lightest touch. Closing her eyes, she was aware of the blood pounding through her, and every fibre was alive to his touch as he drew her closer towards him in an embrace. It was wonderful to be in his arms, her body pressed against his, strong and warm and lovely.

Then he kissed her again, longer this time, and she wanted it never to end.

Chapter Six

1943

As the summer months went on they saw each other often. Mostly, they just walked and talked, making the most of the long days. They saw nothing more of Terry, and Peggy heard through the village grapevine that he had started his residency at the big hospital in Cambridge. She wished him well and was glad that he was far away.

Now and then, Zack came to the Queen's Head in the evenings, sometimes with Freddie and sometimes alone to play a few songs on the piano and snatch snippets of conversation with Peggy as she collected glasses and dishes, so that she worked with a spring in her step and a bigger smile than usual, glowing in the light of his attention. The airbase had not yet started flying live missions, and though the men were busy in the lead-up to their entry into the war, they both knew that these were stolen days, precious and to be treasured.

On a rainy night late in August, she took a moment from clearing tables to sit with Zack at the little table by the hearth that was his usual spot. It was a Tuesday night, and in spite of the season the fire crackled with welcome warmth. The pub was quiet – a couple of regulars propped up the bar, talking about football to her father, who was listening with an interest she knew to be feigned. Once or twice, he cast a glance her way and rolled his eyes, making her smile. In the far corner, her friend Sylvia was deep in conversation with her new man, an airman Zack had said he only knew by sight when Peggy asked him. His name was Jim, Sylvia had told her, and he was a gunner too. They looked happy and in love, she thought, as she watched them, eyes only for each other. Then she wondered if she and Zack looked the same way when they were together. She guessed that perhaps they did.

Zack took her hand and held it on the bench between them. She sensed straight away his nervousness, the hesitation in what he was about to say. Her heart seemed to turn in her chest with the fear of bad news to come.

'What is it?' she asked. 'What's wrong?'

'Nothing's wrong,' he was quick to assure her. 'Nothing at all. It's just …' He lowered his head away from her for a moment, searching the floor of the pub as if for inspiration. Then he lifted his eyes to meet hers and held them steady in a gaze she could not have looked away from for a million pounds. 'I have a seventy-two-hour pass coming up in a couple of weeks,' he said. 'I was thinking of going somewhere – maybe London. I've never been, and I was, well, I … was wondering if you'd be able to come with me.'

Fear transmuted swiftly into relief and delight.

'Of course I'll come,' she said, without hesitation. 'Of course.'

'Your father won't mind?'

'I'm twenty-four years old.'

'I know. But you're still his daughter. I don't want to cause any trouble between you.'

She hesitated. Her father had rarely refused her anything (her mother used to say that he was wound around her little finger) and she had never needed to lie to him before. But as Zack said, she was still his daughter, his little girl. Would he approve of a weekend away with an American airman? Even with Zack, who he liked? Would he give her his blessing? It was a lot to ask, after all. She let the thought curl around her mind, considering. In spite of the independence he had always allowed her and the new world the war had ushered in, in many ways the old standards had not changed at all: nice girls didn't spend the weekend with men who were not their husbands.

She cast another glance towards her father, who was still trapped at the bar talking about the football. He would think less of her, and of Zack too, and it was this last thought that decided her – she did not want to disappoint him.

'We won't tell him,' she said, and wrapped her fingers more tightly in his.

She saw the flicker of concern in Zack's eyes, the doubt. 'Are you sure? What'll you say to him?'

'I'll think of something. Don't worry.'

'I like your dad,' he murmured. 'I don't want you to lie to him on my account.'

He seemed a little in awe of her father, comparing him perhaps to his own, the man he had rejected at a young age for his drunkeness and violence. 'You could have your own room.'

'What if I don't want my own room?'

He laughed then and slid his eyes away from hers, made shy by the promise those words contained.

'Then that would be fine,' he answered, after a moment. 'More than fine, in fact.'

The clock on the mantel above the fire struck nine, and both of them looked towards it, counting the chimes.

'I gotta go,' Zack said, standing up.

'I'll see you out,' she replied, and followed him to the door.

Outside, he wrapped her in his arms, drawing her close, and she was conscious of the warmth of his chest against hers, the hard muscles of his thighs and his arms as he held her. When she tilted her head upwards for his kiss, heat flared through every part of her with a new passion and desire she had not allowed herself to feel until now. An image of a hotel room flittered through her thoughts – the two of them together, limbs entwined, the weight of his body on hers. She let her thoughts linger on the image, growing warm with the pleasure of it, and with a delightful new awareness of the man beneath the clothes – skin and muscle and sinew, blood and bone – she wanted him completely.

The street was dark: the lamp that hung over the door to the pub had been unlit since the war began, and the air was soft with the last remnants of the evening's rain, cool against her face. She wished for more light so that she could see the face of this man she loved, and answer the hunger she knew was in his eyes with desire of her own. Her breath lifted, heavy with want for him, and as they kissed, she knew he too was thinking of that hotel bed in London, when they could be together truly.

Somewhere out of sight an engine stuttered into life and cut the silence, and the sudden sound brought her thoughts back to the high street: her father in the pub behind them, and the long walk back to the base for Zack. An automatic sense of guilt for her thoughts suffused her and she felt the redness flush across her skin. Biting her lip, she stepped back from his embrace with reluctance, and the night was suddenly cold without his warmth against her.

'I'll see you soon,' he murmured, and turned to go.

She listened to the trudge of his boots on the wet road as he set off on his way through the village and hugged herself against the cool of the night. But when his footsteps waned into silence and she stepped back inside the pub, she thought again of the waiting hotel room in London and could not keep the smile from her face.

The next day brought fine weather – a brisk breeze had washed the sky clear of the last of the clouds, and the sun beat brightly on the puddles in the road, almost blinding her as she struggled to steer the old bicycle around the ruts. It was a pleasant ride to the Lancasters' farm, delivering pasties for the workers who were busy drilling the sugar beet, and on the way back she stopped at the post office where Sylvia worked.

She arrived just as her friend was turning the sign to *Closed for Lunch*, and Sylvia looked up in delighted surprise to see her – they spent far too little time together these days, spare hours hard to find. But in spite of it their friendship had never waned, and each time they met it was as if no time had passed at all.

They walked together through to the back of the shop and upstairs to the little kitchen above. Sylvia had worked in the post office with her mother since her father joined up not long after war began. He was serving somewhere in North Africa now, and they heard from him only rarely, intermittent letters that were chatty and full of good humour but that revealed precious little of his experiences. Her friend seldom mentioned it but Peggy knew the worry ate at her nerves – she could not imagine how she would feel if her own father had been so far away for so long, at war.

Sylvia made a pot of tea and Peggy set out the two pasties she had saved onto plates. Sitting at the table as they had done so many times through all the years they had known each other, Peggy cast her eyes over the familiar kitchen, taking in the great dresser with its clutter of plates and dishes and ornaments, stacks of cards and photographs, and the pans that hung from the rack above the kerosene stove. She took a mouthful of tea. It was strong and bitter, just how she liked it.

'I need your help,' she said.

Sylvia set down her cup and leaned forward, eyes bright with interest beneath the dark arched eyebrows that Peggy had always envied. Now that she was here, she hesitated, unsure exactly what it was she wanted to ask.

'Zack has asked me to go to London with him the weekend after next. He has a seventy-two-hour pass.'

Her friend grinned and clapped her hands lightly together. 'That's wonderful!'

'Ye-es,' Peggy agreed, 'it is. And I'm very excited about it. Except ...' She paused briefly, a small part of her still unwilling to commit to the deception until the image of the hotel room flickered once more through her thoughts and she found her resolve. 'I don't want Dad to know.'

'Oh.' Sylvia sat back in her chair and let her gaze drift to the window as if the solution might be written in the sky beyond. 'I see.' She turned back, her pale face serious. 'Are you wanting an alibi?'

'I don't know,' Peggy sighed. 'I mean, you work in the post office – I can't say I was with you all weekend if you're here.'

'I could come with you,' Sylvia suggested, 'as your chaperone.' She giggled, and Peggy shot her a look of irritation.

'This is serious.'

Her friend sobered. 'I know,' she said gently. 'And I know how hard it is to get time alone with your man in a place like this.'

'How do you and Jim manage?' She knew without doubt that Sylvia would have found a way. With her curves and filmstar looks, she had never made a secret of her relationships, often recounting them to Peggy in shocking detail. But she seemed unusually serious about Jim and Peggy was pleased for her.

Sylvia gestured with her head towards the back door.

'Dad's Ford Prefect in the garage. It's just been sitting there since he went away – there's no petrol, even if I could drive it. May as well use it for something.' She arched one of her beautiful eyebrows and gave a coy shrug, and Peggy couldn't help but laugh.

'It doesn't sound very comfortable,' she said, thinking again of the imagined hotel in London with its warm, soft bed, and her body intertwined with Zack's; sweet perfection.

'It's not,' her friend agreed. 'But you have to make do, don't you? Where else are we going to go?'

There was a silence and they ate their pasties. Somewhere outside a tractor started up, shattering the afternoon stillness, and a dog barked in response.

'Seriously, though, I could come with you if you want,'

Sylvia said again, after a while. 'And then leave you to it once we get there.'

Peggy stared at her – it seemed an awful lot to ask.

'What would you do with yourself?'

'I've got a cousin in London I haven't seen for ages. We could say you were coming with me to see her? I'll have to talk to Mum – it means she'll have the shop on her own. But I'm sure she'll be fine. I haven't been anywhere for … I can't remember the last time.'

'That's ever so good of you,' she said. 'Are you sure you wouldn't mind? I never expected you to do that – I just came to ask if you had any ideas—'

Sylvia cut her off with a laugh. 'Of course I don't mind. You'd do the same for me. Besides, it'll be rather fun. I like my cousin, even if she is a bit of a bluestocking, and it's always exciting to get away for a weekend, especially to London.'

Peggy nodded her agreement. And in spite of her misgivings about the scale of the deception, it seemed like the beginnings of a plan.

Chapter Seven

1943

The days until the weekend in London dragged past and every single hour felt like an age. Peggy was terrified she would let the secret slip, or that her father would see through her story to the truth beneath: though she had no doubts about being with Zack, the guilt still niggled inside. Her father would be heartbroken to know she had lied to him, but she simply couldn't bear to tell the truth and see the look of disappointment in his eyes. He would think less of her, and of Zack. He might possibly forbid her to go. At heart, he was an old-fashioned man – nice girls waited until they were married – and she was his only daughter.

Finally, the day arrived, and she could hardly keep the smile from her face, an unaccustomed spring in her step. Twice during the morning she caught her father's curious glance, but it was no secret she was going to London with her friend and so she had every right to be excited. Even so, she was still afraid he would discern the truth somehow, and it was only when she stepped out of the pub door to make her way to the train station at last that the fear began to diminish.

They caught the afternoon train, and she felt like a child on a long-promised adventure, chatting excitedly with Sylvia as Zack watched the passing English countryside beyond the dirty window. But even as she chattered with her friend, Peggy's hand remained tightly laced in his, and their bodies were close on the bench, brushing now and then with the movement of the train.

It was a long trip with two changes of train, and the carriages were full to bursting with British and Americans in uniform vying for seats with civilians from all walks of life. But for once there were no delays and they arrived in London late in the evening, drawing into the city through the dark of the blackout, so that it was impossible to know just where they were. Zack peered into the night.

'See anything?' Sylvia asked.

He shook his head and gave her a rueful smile. But he did not shift his gaze away, as though if he only looked for long enough the city would coalesce into shapes he could recognise.

'I've wanted to visit London my whole life,' he said. 'I had a picture book as a kid with picture of Big Ben and the Tower of London, and I promised myself that one day I'd see them for real.'

'And so you shall,' Sylvia laughed.

He turned briefly from the dark of the window. 'I still can't get my head around the history – buildings that predate the founding of America, a city that dates from Roman times.'

Peggy squeezed his hand, his delight infectious, and when the train pulled into Liverpool Street with a great hiss of steam, they stepped down together beneath the cavernous roof where whistles and voices echoed beneath the great iron girders. The station was softly lit with a glow that glimmered through the steam, rendering the platform strange and other-worldly. Pausing for a moment on the platform to get their bearings, they looked around them through the half-light. Across the tracks, they could see the far wall had been shattered by German bombs, jagged edges and the roof open to the sky. Zack squeezed Peggy's hand a little tighter and they exchanged a glance that held too many meanings to give them voice.

Outside the station they halted, disorientated by the black-out. Shadows moved like ghosts along the street and Peggy took her little torch from her handbag to light the pavement at their feet. A cab pulled up, its headlights no more than slits that barely penetrated the dark.

'This is me,' Sylvia said, and with a hug for Peggy and a smile for Zack that he might not even have seen in the dark, she opened the door and got in. 'See you tomorrow,' she called back, before she slammed the door. 'Have fun!'

The taxi pulled away and was quickly swallowed by the night. They stood closer together, fingers still intertwined. Another taxi purred to the kerb, and they got in. Zack gave the cabbie the name of a small hotel near Paddington that one of his crew had recommended, and it seemed like a long way as the taxi moved slowly through the bomb-cratered streets. Peggy peered out of the windows, trying to see where they were going, but all the streets seemed the same in the darkness and nothing was familiar – they could have been anywhere. Giving up the struggle she turned away from the window – the route through the city had been no more than a distraction anyway from the thoughts in her head and the pleasure of the sensations in her body. Her heart was pattering in her chest with nerves and excitement, her hand still caught in Zack's, and now and then she sensed more than saw him turn his head to smile to her through the gloom.

Finally, the cab pulled up and the driver turned in his seat to speak to them.

'This is it,' he said.

They got out and looked around them. The hotel was in a side street, a Victorian terrace in a long row of similar buildings with columns either side of the door and large windows covered with the usual criss-crossed tape. Peggy flicked a glance along the road to look for bomb damage, but from what she could see through the dark the row still seemed to be complete, as yet untouched by the Germans.

They turned to each other on the pavement, caught in the pleasure of the moment. She was aware of Zack's closeness and the touch of his fingers in hers, his warmth, and her blood seemed to quiver in her veins. She could hardly believe she was really here at last – she had imagined this moment so many times.

'Are you ready?' Zack asked.

'Absolutely,' she replied.

Then they turned and walked up the couple of steps and into the hotel lobby.

'I have a room booked for Mr and Mrs Eldon,' Zack told the elderly clerk at the reception desk, and Peggy's heart quickened a little more at the sound of it.

Peggy Eldon. She ran the feel of it across her tongue and decided that she liked it.

The clerk looked them up and down with disapproval, unconvinced, and she guessed he saw a lot of couples and servicemen, married and otherwise. But he held his peace – it was not his job to dish out moral judgements but to take the guests' money – and simply handed Zack the key to their room without a word.

'Third floor. The dining room is closed,' he told them, as though it were their fault. 'But the bar is open, if you would like a drink. Hot water comes on at six a.m. Breakfast is from half past.'

They took the key and headed for the stairs, Peggy following behind as Zack carried their bags. The room was at the end of a dimly lit corridor and when they opened the door and switched on the light, they stood just inside for a moment, blinking in the sudden brightness. It was a modest room but clean and bright, with a large double bed and a window that in the daytime she guessed would look out over the garden at the back of the hotel. For now, heavy wool curtains of an indeterminate colour shut out the night. There was a washbasin in the corner, and they had passed the bathroom on their way along the corridor.

Zack put down the bags and crossed to the nightstand to turn on the lamp. Peggy switched off the too-bright overhead light with relief so that the room was suddenly bathed in a soft golden glow. There was a silence. They smiled at each other, self-conscious now, and awkward. From outside she was aware of the hum of the city – the rumble of distant traffic, an airplane passing overhead, and somewhere, far away, the faint wail of a siren. It was years since she had been to London – a school trip, she recalled, to the British Museum – and after the peace of Sutton Heath, the noise was disconcerting.

'Should we go down to the bar for a drink?' Zack asked.

'Yes,' she agreed. 'Let's.'

Now that she was here at last in the room she had dreamt of for so long, the heat of her desire was tempered by a sudden rush of nervousness. It was not quite as she had imagined: she had pictured herself as self-assured, confident with her man. But instead, all the nerves of her innocence seemed to crowd inside her, and the customary ease of being with Zack deserted her completely. Would he still like her after this? Would he still want her? She looked at him, handsome in the glow of the table lamp, turning his service cap lightly between his fingers, watching her, and thought she barely knew him at all.

'Are you okay?' His voice was soft, gentle.

'I ... don't know,' she answered.

'Hey, it's all right,' he said, and came towards her, taking her hand in his, caressing the fingers as he drew her closer to him. 'Are you having second thoughts?'

She shook her head, furious with herself for her doubts.

'No,' she said quickly. 'Not at all. It's just strange and I'm nervous and it isn't at all what I thought it would be.' The words tumbled over one another, barely making sense, and she lowered her head away, embarrassed to meet his gaze.

He tucked a strand of hair behind her shoulder as he had done so many times before, but this time it felt unbearably intimate and she shivered.

'What did you think it would be like?'

'I don't know. I thought ... I thought I'd feel different somehow.'

'What kind of different?'

He was standing very close to her so that she could feel the warmth of his body, almost touching. His fingers reached for hers again, caressing them lightly.

'I didn't think I'd be so nervous. I've imagined this moment so many times in my head, and I was always sexy and sophisticated—'

'You are sexy,' he interrupted. Then he added, 'I don't know about sophisticated though.'

She laughed, and the tightness of the tension unwound a little with the humour.

'But I wouldn't want you to be any different from what you are, right now, here with me. I wouldn't change a single thing about you. You're perfect as you are.'

Tears prickled behind her eyes at his words, and finally she raised her head to look at him.

'And now I've made you cry.' He gave her a rueful smile and drew her closer into him so that her head was resting on his shoulder, her cheek against the wool of his tunic. His arms tightened around her back and she nestled into him, safe and warm in his embrace. With one hand he began to stroke her hair, and she was aware of the touch of his lips against her head. A new warmth rippled through her belly and her breathing quickened.

'Do you still want to get a drink?' he whispered, and she felt the movement of his mouth against her hair.

She shook her head.

'Are you sure?'

She tipped back her head to meet his gaze. Their faces were very close and he was looking right into her, green eyes lit with love and hunger. The warmth inside her flared into heat.

'I'm sure,' she whispered back.

Zack lifted his hand and gently stroked her cheek with the backs of his fingers, and she rubbed her head against his touch. Then he lowered his mouth to hers and kissed her. With the brush of his lips on hers, the last vestiges of her shyness slid away. Her whole body was alive and ready for his touch, waiting, wanting. Every fibre cried out for his caress. They moved into each other as they kissed, and he began to unbutton her blouse, reaching inside to cup her breast so that her back arched in pleasure. Breathless, they pulled apart, and began to strip away their own clothes until they were standing almost naked by the bed.

Though the room was warm Peggy shivered, both proud and self-conscious in the flimsy slip that was all that covered her, and she could not tear her eyes away from the lean, muscled body before her, wearing only his trunks, his skin white and taut, a dusting of dark hair across his chest. He was beautiful, she thought, and raised her hand to trace the lines of his muscles with a fingertip across his shoulder and his arms, his chest and his belly. His breath shuddered with her touch, as though he could barely keep balance on his feet.

Her fingers halted at the waistband of his trunks and she looked up at him with a question in her eyes. He smiled, but shook his head.

'Not yet,' he said, and instead reached up to draw the strap of her slip away from her shoulder, lowering his head to kiss the soft skin of her neck. Surprised by the force of the pleasure of it, she held her breath as he lowered the other strap so that the slip fell away into a pool at her feet.

He drew her close to him once again, and this time it was skin to skin, her breasts against his chest, his hardness against her belly as they kissed. With one hand he caressed her, his fingers searching across her skin, lighting a trail of fire in their wake as they found their way across her breasts and belly, around her buttocks and thighs.

Then he shifted back towards the bed and, though she did not want him to stop, she understood as he yanked back the sheets and pulled her towards him so that they both half lay, half fell into the softness. She was aware of everything. The cool smoothness of the sheets beneath her, the warmth of his body next to hers, their legs entwined, the hard muscles of his arms as he lifted himself over her. Without waiting to ask him this time, she reached to lower his trunks down over his hips, and when he entered her it was the most exquisite sensation, pleasure and pain wrapped together – transcendent. He began to move, and she wrapped her legs around him, drawing him deeper and moving with him.

It was over too soon but she knew that it was only the first time, and that there would be many more. A whole lifetime, she hoped. She turned her head towards him beside her, eyes half-closed, still in the lazy aftermath, and he slid his arm around her so that she lay with her head on his shoulder, her finger trailing through the dust of hair, caressing.

They lay in silence a while, content just to be with each other, no need for words when they could talk with the closeness of their bodies, and Peggy was conscious of nothing but his presence and the sweetness of what they had shared.

After a while though, the cold air began to creep across her skin, chilling her, and so she shifted to drag the covers up and over them. The movement broke the silent magic of the moment, and Zack rolled over onto his side to face her.

'I have a question for you,' he whispered.

Their faces were very close on the pillows, their legs interlocked, hands tucked neatly before them, and she thought again how handsome he was, and how lucky they were to have found each other.

'What?' she murmured back. Her mind was still sleepy and sluggish, still floating in the wash of the pleasure, so she didn't even think to wonder what he might ask.

'Will you marry me?'

She stared, taken by surprise. In this night already full of wonders she could not have imagined this and in her hesitation she saw the fear flicker through his eyes that he had asked too much, too soon.

'I mean, only ...' he stammered.

'Of course I'll marry you,' she said quickly. 'Of course. Of course. You just surprised me. I wasn't expecting it.'

'I don't have a ring yet.'

'It doesn't matter.'

'I thought we could get one here in London, together, so you can pick out something you like.'

'I would love that,' she replied. She was laughing with delight and surprise, and the tears streamed down her face.

Then Zack laughed too, until after a moment he leaned over to kiss her and made love to her again.

Chapter Eight

1943

They had arranged to meet Sylvia and her cousin for dinner the next night at a little restaurant in a cellar in Camden near the cousin's house. It was smoky and crowded with servicemen, and they had to wait a long time for their table even though they had booked. Sylvia made the introductions and they sat in a seat by the window drinking beer out of bottles while they waited.

'I miss having wine,' Sylvia lamented, and her cousin Judy, who was a scholarly-looking woman with glasses and her hair drawn back too tightly in a bun, nodded her agreement. 'Jim can get wine,' Sylvia went on, with a questioning look at Zack, as if he too should be able to.

Black market, Peggy assumed. Even at the pub, they could only rarely get wine.

'I don't drink wine.' Zack shrugged and exchanged a small smile with Peggy, who had to fight to suppress a laugh. She was still giddy with excitement, walking on air, though she could not have said which had made her happier – his proposal, the love they had shared that came before it, or the day they had spent together wandering through London and seeing the sights – Big Ben, the Tower of London, Trafalgar Square and the National Gallery.

Absently, she twiddled the ring he had bought her that afternoon around her finger. It was an antique ruby with two tiny diamonds from a second-hand shop they discovered by chance in a lane not far from the station. Sylvia hadn't yet noticed it, and Peggy wanted to wait until they were at their table before she showed it off. She reached for Zack's hand and he held it tightly, their fingers entwined.

At last, the waiter came to take them through and Peggy sat across from Zack, her foot pressed against his under the table. They ordered straight away from the limited menu – shepherd's pie and peas – and Peggy wished that she and Zack were still alone together, somewhere quiet with just the two of them. The cellar echoed with voices, and they could barely hear each other speak above the clamour. Two American airmen passed by and one of them, swaying with alcohol and noticing Zack with three women at his table, leaned in and murmured, 'Greedy bastard – you need to learn to share.' Then he was gone with a laugh, winding his way between the tables towards the door.

Peggy saw the colour rise in Zack's face, his fists clenching on the tabletop as he half rose from his seat, and she reached across to lay her hand on his.

'It isn't worth it,' she said. 'Leave it.'

He hesitated for half a heartbeat before he lowered himself back into his chair with a shake of his head.

'He was just drunk,' she said, and gave him a small smile. For a moment she wondered if he would go after the man after all, his eyes still watching him over her head, cheeks flushed with fury, but then he lowered his gaze and, with an effort, returned her smile.

'Yeah. Just drunk,' he agreed. 'But still ...'

'What did he say?' Sylvia asked, leaning forward to make herself heard.

'Nothing,' Peggy answered. 'He was just a drunk.'

There was a silence, and conversation was hard to find. She was aware of Zack's gaze on her face and the touch of his foot against hers beneath the table, and she wished again that they were alone together, their chatter easy and never-ending. She caught his eye and they exchanged a smile so that she knew he was thinking the same thing.

Then Sylvia noticed Peggy's ring and exclaimed with a cry that caught the attention of the diners at the table next to them.

'Oh my goodness! That's wonderful! Congratulations!' She hugged her friend, then slid from her chair and rounded the table to hug Zack too. He laughed in self-conscious surprise.

'Congratulations,' Judy said.

Sylvia returned to her seat and two British soldiers at a nearby table observed her movements with frank appreciation, but she was oblivious. She reached out to touch the ring, head tilted, beaming as she turned again to face her friend.

'I'm so happy for you,' she said. Then to Zack. 'You'd better take good care of her.'

'I plan to,' he replied, and his fingertips brushed against Peggy's.

'Have you set a date?'

They looked at each other and laughed.

'No,' Peggy said. 'We haven't even thought about it yet.'

And it was true. In the pleasure of each other's company

all through that day – the excitement of his proposal and choosing the ring – it hadn't occurred to either of them to think any further ahead.

'You should,' Sylvia urged. 'You should get married as soon as you can.' Then she asked, 'Are you going to have a church wedding? Can I be your maid of honour?'

Peggy laughed again, her friend's excitement lighting her own, and looked to Zack, who shrugged.

'I don't know,' she said. 'But you'll be the first to know when we decide anything.'

A red-faced waitress brought their food on a tray and put it in front of them before she turned without a word and wove her way between the tables back towards the kitchen.

Sylvia leaned in to Peggy and said in an undertone, 'I'm so jealous. I keep waiting for Jim to pop the question too.'

'Has he hinted that he might?'

'Yes. Several times. And we've talked about the future, going to live in America after the war …' She trailed off with a shrug.

'I'm sure he'll ask soon. He's probably just waiting for the right time.'

'Perhaps,' Sylvia conceded, but she looked unconvinced, her pretty face drawn into a frown.

Zack gave Peggy a questioning look and she returned it with a tilt of her head that said she would tell him later. Then all of them began to eat the tasteless food. They ate far better at home, she thought, where fresh food was more plentiful. The shortages were much worse in the city.

They finished their meal and headed out into the more peaceful dark of the street. Peggy was relieved to be out of the racket of the restaurant – the street was quiet with few people about. An elderly man with a small dog on a piece of string walked past them, his torch lowered to the pavement before his feet. The dog paused to regard them with soft brown eyes until the man gave the string a gentle tug, and it trotted on. They stood in an awkward group and Peggy shifted closer to Zack, who took her hand and squeezed it.

'It was nice to meet you,' Zack said to Judy.

'You too,' she answered. 'I'm sorry the restaurant wasn't nicer – it used to be good.'

'It was okay,' he said, with a good-natured shrug.

'Where are you two off to now?' Sylvia asked.

'I don't know,' Peggy replied. 'We'll think of something.'

For a moment no one spoke and there was another awkward pause before Sylvia took her leave with a promise to see them both at the station the following afternoon. They watched the two women as they moved off down the street, their little torch barely piercing the gloom.

Later, settled comfortably in the plush seats of the deserted hotel bar, they ordered tea. In another world they would have ordered champagne to celebrate their news, but instead they clinked their teacups together with a laugh. She didn't mind the lack of champagne – in another world they would not have met, and it seemed like a small price to pay.

'What did Sylvia whisper to you in the restaurant?' he asked.

'She's hoping Jim will ask her to marry him soon too. They've been together since January. He was one of the first to arrive.'

Zack made no reply but took a deep breath instead and let his gaze wander across the bar as though lost in thought.

'What is it?' Peggy asked, and he turned back to her abruptly.

'He isn't going to ask her to marry him.'

'How can you know that? I thought you hardly knew him.'

'Because he's already married,' he said. 'He has a wife back home, a couple of kids …' He trailed off and took a mouthful of tea, watching her reaction over the rim of the cup.

'But …' She stopped. It made no sense. They were in love, she was certain. She had seen them together, so right for each other. And Sylvia had talked about him so often, and with such affection, she felt as though she knew him too. Surely Zack was mistaken. 'Are you sure?'

He nodded. 'He was in the mess the other day, showing some of the other guys photos of his kids that his wife had just sent. He put them away when I showed up, but I saw enough to know what they were.'

Peggy said nothing, her heart heavy with pain for her friend. She was going to be devastated.

'Are you going to tell her?'

'I'll have to,' she said, reluctantly. 'I don't want to, though.' Then she had a thought: 'Perhaps he plans to leave his wife for her? It's possible, isn't it?'

'Even so, is that the kind of man you want for her? That would leave his wife and kids on the other side of the world for another woman?'

She shook her head, and the shine of the evening with Zack seemed to dim a little with this unwelcome news. She looked up at him with a surge of doubt.

'You don't have a wife in America too, do you?' she said, but as soon as the words were out of her mouth she regretted them. She saw the hurt that flickered in his eyes, the tension in his jaw.

'I'm sorry,' she whispered quickly. 'I didn't mean that. I truly didn't. I'm sorry, Zack.'

'You don't trust me?'

'Of course I do,' she answered, and laid her hand on top of his on the table. In the lamplight the ruby glittered, but he didn't take her fingers as he usually did. She could feel the weight of his gaze on her face as he watched, as though seeing her anew. Terrified her words had ruined everything, she spoke again, words almost tripping over themselves trying to repair the damage.

'I'm sorry,' she said again. 'I just love you so much and I'm so happy we're together, that I'm terrified of anything that might come between us, anything that could spoil it all. Of course I trust you. I just had a moment of doubt because of Jim, a moment of dread.' She searched his face, desperate, and for the first time couldn't read what she saw there. 'Please tell me you still love me.' His eyes were lowered to the table, and she waited, barely breathing, heartbeat quick with fear. After a moment that felt like an age, he lifted his head and met her gaze with eyes that were shadowed with a sadness she had not seen before.

'Of course I still love you,' he said. He shifted his hand on the table and took her fingers in his at last. 'We've played "As Time Goes By" together, and that makes us partners, remember? You're not going to get rid of me that easily.' He smiled, and though her eyes were blurred with tears, she smiled in return.

'I'm so sorry,' she whispered once more. 'I don't know why I said it.'

'I do,' he replied. 'I come from a different world, far away, and you can't know what my life was like before I got here. You only have my word for it, and you just agreed to tie your life to mine. That's a big leap of faith.'

She nodded, unable to bring words to her tongue, the tears too close to the surface to speak. Instead she caressed his fingers, and hoped he understood. They sat for a while without talking but the silence was comfortable again, and they were at ease with each other. The last of the tea grew cold, and finally Zack said, 'Shall we go upstairs?'

She nodded and stood up, then took his hand and followed him up the narrow staircase. By the time they reached their room, all her doubts were forgotten.

Chapter Nine

1943

They caught the homeward train late in the afternoon and though Sylvia chatted on about the day she had spent exploring London with her aunt and uncle, the lovers were quiet with each other, content just to be in each other's company. But the truth about Sylvia's sweetheart weighed heavily on Peggy's conscience, and as the train rattled through the growing dark, the passing landscape unseen beyond the windows, she tried to think how she might best break the news. With each possibility, her guts contracted anew in dread – there was no easy way to say it, no right time, and she was aware that her friend might not even believe her, that telling her could damage their friendship forever. She would have to pick her moment with care.

She leaned closer into Zack's shoulder, savouring his warmth, dozing now and then and abstractedly playing with the ring on her finger. She would need to take it off before she got home, she thought, and a ripple of guilt ran through her at the lie she had told her father and for all the other lies she would have to tell him in the future.

They changed trains at Cambridge, stepping down on to the platform into a bitter wind that whipped through the station and grabbed at her hair and the hem of her coat. They found the waiting room but it was already full. Every inch of seating was already taken – mothers with children, servicemen, workers, and an elderly couple with a cat in a cage. There had been delays, as there always were, and the station was crowded with cold, bored passengers awaiting trains they should have boarded hours ago.

They went instead to the cafeteria and found a last empty table in the corner. Zack bought tea for them all, and they sat close together on the bench. Though the tea was weak and only lukewarm, it was good to have something to do and as she sipped at it, Peggy let her eyes wander across the other passengers. Some British airmen were playing cards in a group near the counter, and the young girl who was serving kept sliding worried glances their way. A pair of businessmen were engaged in earnest discussion, and a vicar sat reading his Bible. A mother was reading a book to her two children, who looked bored and tired, but they were quiet, for which Peggy was grateful. The emotions and sleeplessness of the weekend were beginning to tell – she could have curled up quite happily in Zack's embrace and slept like a child herself.

The bell on the door gave a tinkle, and a rush of cold air made the passengers shiver as the door opened and closed. A well-dressed young man entered, a hat low down over his head, and when he lifted his hand to take it off she saw with a rush of horror that it was Terry. Panic welled inside her and she buried her face in Zack's shoulder, but it was too late. Terry had recognised Sylvia, and he was already on his away across the floor towards them.

She felt Zack brace beside her, muscles tensing and breath becoming quick, and she laid a warning hand on his arm.

'Don't,' she whispered. 'He's not worth it.'

'I'm not going to do anything,' Zack murmured in reply.

'Terry!' Sylvia was the first to greet him, and she flashed him her most brilliant smile. 'How lovely to see you. Are you on your way home?'

'Yes. My mother isn't well.'

'I'm so sorry to hear that,' Peggy said, and meant it. As the local doctor's wife, Mrs Anderson had tended in one way or another to most of the village at some time in their lives. She was a reserved and quiet woman who kept her thoughts to herself, and she was well-liked by everyone. 'I hope it isn't serious?'

'Hopefully not.' He looked around for a stool or a chair, even though he had not been invited to join them, but there were none spare that he could see. Undeterred, he kept up the conversation. 'And where have you been to find yourself at Cambridge station on a windy Sunday night?'

'We went to London for the weekend, to see Sylvia's cousin,' Peggy replied.

'Him too?' He lifted his chin towards Zack, who never took his eyes off the newcomer. Peggy could feel the latent aggression in the hardness of his muscles under her palm.

'Me too,' Zack confirmed.

There was a pause. Then Terry, perhaps recalling his manners, said, 'Can I get anyone more tea?'

Peggy shook her head.

'Sylvia?'

'No, thank you.'

'I will,' Zack said. 'Thanks.'

Peggy flicked him a glance that was somewhere between irritation and laughter, and her hand pressed down more firmly on his arm. Briefly meeting her look, he put his own hand on hers, and she remembered she was still wearing the ring. She wondered if Terry had noticed it yet.

While Terry was at the counter, a train pulled in and the RAF party packed up their cards and hurried to the door. Peggy slipped the ring from her finger and put it on the chain at her neck so that it sat alongside the little St Christopher she always wore. She should give the St Christopher to Zack, she thought, to keep him safe when he finally began his journeys over Europe. Next time they were alone together, she thought. For now, she tucked the necklace inside the neck of her blouse and did up an extra button to hide it.

Terry returned with one of the stools the airmen had left, and tea for himself and for Zack.

'Thank you,' Zack said. Then he held out his hand to shake the other man's. 'Zack Eldon. I think we got off on the wrong foot before.'

Terry hesitated, and perhaps if Peggy had not been there his reaction might have been different. But after a long moment he extended his own hand and grasped the airman's.

'Terry Anderson.'

They shook, once, briefly, and the look that passed between them still shimmered with hostility, but Peggy was relieved that at least they were not at each other's throats. She tried not to think about the fallout from their meeting. She knew Terry would tell her father, and her secret would be out. Terry settled himself on the stool and grimaced at the first mouthful of tea.

'I don't know how they can serve this muck as tea,' he grumbled. 'We get a better brew at the hospital.'

'Are you enjoying it there?' Sylvia turned all her attention towards him, doing her best to smooth out the tension.

'It's hard work,' he replied. 'Long hours and all that. But I'm learning a lot, so yes, I suppose I'm enjoying it, though it isn't what I want to do in the long term.'

'What do you want to do?'

'Surgery,' he replied without hesitation.

'Not a family doctor with your dad?' Peggy asked, surprised by his answer. Growing up he had always talked about joining his father, the two men working side by side, a family practice.

He shook his head. 'I've more ambition than that, and I'd like to live in the city. I've developed quite a taste for it through the years at university. More to feed the mind there, and more to do. Sutton Heath is a bit of a backwater really.'

Peggy bridled at his condescension, biting her lip against the answers that gathered behind it.

'I kinda like it,' Zack said.

'Well, you would,' Terry replied, and opened his mouth to say more, but Zack cut him off.

'And if you want to live in a city you should try New York. That's where we're going to live after the war.' He turned to Peggy. 'Isn't that right, honey?'

'Yes. I can't wait.' She smiled, but inside she was uncertain if he truly meant it or if he was saying it merely to goad Terry. They hadn't spoken much of their plans for the future.

'I mean, I'm sure Cambridge is nice, but it's not much compared to New York. Or even London.'

The muscle in Terry's jaw began to twitch, and the hand

that rested on the table in front of him balled into a fist. He was breathing hard with ill-suppressed fury.

'Does your father know you're planning to run away with an American?' he asked, turning his attention to Peggy.

She sighed. Whatever she said, she knew it was going to end badly. 'Terry, can we please just enjoy our cup of tea while we wait for the train? We've had a lovely weekend, and I don't want to spoil it by arguing with you.'

Terry dropped his eyes to his teacup and turned it lightly to and fro in its saucer. He said nothing.

'We've been friends a long time,' she continued. 'Let's not ruin it now.'

With a long deep breath, he nodded. But he didn't shift his gaze from the cup, still turning it to and fro, to and fro.

Peggy lifted her head to look at Zack, who met her eyes with an expression she couldn't read.

An announcement came over the loudspeaker and everyone in the cafeteria cocked their heads to listen.

'That's us,' Sylvia said, getting up and sliding into her coat. Then, to Terry, who was still staring at the table, she asked, 'Are you getting the same train?'

'Yes, but I'm travelling first class.'

'Of course! I should have known,' Sylvia said brightly, with a laugh. 'Well, in that case, we'll see you at home.'

He got up and, with a curt nod to Peggy, turned on his heel and went out on to the platform. When they followed a moment later, he was nowhere to be seen in the dark.

Chapter Ten

1943

There was no sign of Terry on the platform when they got down from the train to change to the branch line, and though Peggy briefly wondered where he'd gone, the feeling didn't last long, subsumed by a sense of profound relief that she would not have to talk to him again. At least not yet.

The guard told them they had missed their connection and that there would be no more trains that night.

'You can wait in the waiting room, if you like,' he said, 'Or there's a pub in the village that has rooms to rent.' He glanced at the station clock. 'It's a bit late, but I expect they'll still be up.'

'I don't want to sleep in the waiting room,' Zack said. 'If I liked sleeping rough I'd have joined the army.'

Peggy laughed, switched on her torch, and they set off, all three of them arm in arm, to find the pub the guard told them was on the village high street.

. . .

Later, when they were lying alongside each other in the soft hotel bed, skin against skin, she stroked the strong muscles of his arm, tracing the lines of them, still in awe that she could and full of wonder at his beauty. Sylvia, in a room along the hall, was utterly forgotten.

'Did you mean what you said?' she asked. 'About living in New York?'

'If you want to,' he replied. 'You said you wanted to go there. Or we can stay here. Wherever you want to go. I only said it to wind Terry up.'

'It certainly worked.' She smiled, and he touched his fingers to her lips, their faces close together.

'Is he really your friend?'

'He's not so bad. You just seem to bring out the worst in him. It's jealousy, I suppose. I never realised quite how much he liked me. He's never asked me out or anything. Never even suggested the possibility.'

'Maybe he was waiting till he was qualified, so that he could sweep you off your feet to be a doctor's wife. He seems like the kind of guy who might think like that – all his *i's* dotted and his *t's* crossed before he does anything. Nothing left to chance.'

'I think you might be right,' she replied. Now she came to think of it, Zack's blunt assessment of Terry was deadly accurate. She thought back over all the years she had known him – his commitment to his study, his sober reflections on almost every subject under the sun.

'It's no way to live,' he went on. 'Life is too short. Life is now. If you wait until the perfect time to do anything you'll be waiting forever.'

'I've had a wonderful weekend,' she murmured, touching

her fingers to the ring on the chain at her neck. 'And I'm glad we missed our connection.'

'Me too. This is a much softer bed than the one at the base.'

'Zack!'

He laughed. 'And the company is nicer too,' he added. 'However much I love Freddie, I gotta admit I'd rather spend the night with you.'

'I'm very glad to hear it.'

He grew serious then, and stroked her hair back from her face, tucking it neatly behind her ear. His fingers brushed against her cheekbone, raising a flush of pleasure across her skin. Then he tilted her chin up towards him a little more and kissed her.

It was still early morning when they arrived back in the high street at Sutton Heath, and Zack whispered a quick farewell before he left for the base: if he hurried, he had just enough time to get there within the hours of his pass. The two women embraced, and Peggy watched her friend for a moment as she headed along the street towards the post office.

It was a soft September day. The blustery wind of the previous night had tempered into a breeze, and ragged clouds sailed swiftly overhead across a bright blue sky. Two land girls were chatting in the street, and they smiled in greeting when they saw her. The baker's boy glided past on his bicycle with an empty basket. A normal Monday morning in the village, and after the racket of London the peace was welcome. She thought of Terry's casual disdain for the slowness of its ways and Zack's instinctive defence of it. Then she wondered if she would like New York – it was hard for her to imagine herself living in London even, becoming accustomed to the busy-ness and noise, confident in the traffic and on the tube. But with Zack, she thought, she could go anywhere and be happy. Smiling to herself at the thought of it, she fingered the ring on the chain beside the St Christopher at her neck and turned to go into the pub.

Her father was seated at the one of the tables near the hearth, paperwork strewn in front of him. He looked up at her entrance with a sigh, but brightened briefly when he saw it was her.

'The train was delayed,' she told him. 'And we missed our connection ...' She gave him a small smile and shrug of apology. 'I'll get started on lunch right away.'

'I'm glad you're back, love,' he replied. 'Old Lancaster dropped off a load of vegetables first thing – they're on the back step.' Then he lowered his head once more to the paperwork. She watched him for a moment, noticing the first fine threads of grey at his temples, lines wearing across his forehead, which was creased in concentration. Before the war her mother had always kept the books – one more way in which the shadow of her ghost fell across their lives. A sliver of guilt filtered from her guts: she had never wanted to add to his troubles, and though a small part of her hoped against hope that Terry would keep her secret, she guessed it was only a matter of time before he spilled it. She had seen the way he had looked at them, his disdain and jealousy clear in his face. With a sigh, she forced the thought of it to the back of her mind and went through to the kitchen.

With *Music While You Work* playing softly on the radio set, she worked quickly to prepare the lunches – vegetable pasties and a soup that was seasoned with fresh herbs from the garden – and her thoughts were soon utterly absorbed in the many tasks of cooking. She loved the physical feel of the food-stuffs in her hands – the soft crumbs of pastry, the cold leaves of the vegetables, the grease of the butter – and she was grateful for the way the work seemed to empty her mind of all other concerns.

When the pasties were finally in the oven and the soup was simmering on the stove, she began to clear up, stacking the bowls and plates ready to serve, the cutlery neatly bundled and waiting. Allowing her mind to wander back at last across the weekend in London, she was aware of the ring on its chain at her neck. The metal was warm against her breast-bone, and the memory of the nights they had spent together brought a wave of heat across her skin, a flicker of warmth in her belly. She smiled to herself at the promise of a whole life of nights like that one – warm in Zack's embrace, content simply to be near him.

With a smile to herself, she stepped back through into the bar. She wasn't expecting to see any customers. It was only just past midday and Mondays were always quiet, so it took her a moment to notice Terry seated at the bar, deep in conversation with her father. They both turned at her entrance, and from the abrupt halt in their conversation she knew straight away they were talking about her. Her father slid his eyes away from her, awkward in a way that was unfamiliar. But Terry's gaze remained fixed on her, and she couldn't read the expression on his face.

'I was just telling your dad how we bumped into each other at the station last night.'

She said nothing. It came as no surprise to see him – in her heart she had known from the first moment she saw him in the railway café that he would report back to her father. But that one small part of her had still clung to the hope that the years of their friendship might count for something. Apparently not.

'You and Sylvia and your airman.' He glanced towards her father with a tilt of his head, drained off his pint, and headed for the door. 'I'll leave you two to talk.'

Then he was gone and she was alone with her father in the empty bar.

'Is it true?' her father asked. 'You spent the weekend with Zack Eldon?'

She nodded, eyes lowered, feeling like a child again.

'Why did you lie to me about it?'

'I didn't want you to worry.'

She looked up and moved closer, settling herself on one of the stools at the bar. He picked up a glass and, though it looked perfectly clear to her, he began to polish it automatically with the tea towel that was always in his hand.

'I worry when you lie to me,' he said, without looking up. 'Was it his idea not to tell me? Did he put you up to it?'

'No,' she said quickly. 'It was my idea. He wanted to ask your permission.'

She should have let him, she thought now. But she had been afraid of her father's disapproval, that he would think less of Zack. And even more afraid he would have forbidden her to go.

Her father said nothing and rubbed at an imaginary mark on the glass, and as she waited, all the joy of the weekend seemed to leach out of her so that all she could feel was the disappointment in herself she could see in her father's expression. After a long moment, he set down the glass and picked up another, regarded it briefly, then finally lifted his head to look at her.

'I know you think you're in love with Zack. I can see why you might – he's an attractive young man with his smart bright uniform and his accent. And he's a talented musician, I'll give him that. But the stories I'm hearing about the Americans and the way they treat British girls …' He trailed off and returned to polishing the glass.

'What stories?' she pressed.

'Terry said his father is looking after numerous young women who've found themselves in the family way to Americans who had promised them the world and then abandoned them.' He paused, then looked at her again across the width of the bar.

'Has he said he'll take you back to America after the war? Has he promised you that?'

Peggy felt the pressure of building tears in her throat and behind her eyes.

'And what did he get in return, eh? What did you get up to when you were having a good time in London?'

'He's not like that,' she insisted.

But she thought of Sylvia and Jim, and her friend's belief in the goodness of her man. She supposed that each and every one of those women who had been abandoned were at one time convinced that their lover was a good man who loved them.

'How can you be sure?' her father demanded.

'We're getting married,' she told him. It wasn't how she had planned to break the news, and she wished she didn't have to say it now, in anger like this, but he needed to know so that he would trust Zack with her heart as she did.

'Really?' Her father was unconvinced. 'Given you a ring, has he?'

'Yes,' she said, pulling it out from under her blouse and fumbling to undo the chain so that she might put it on her finger where it belonged.

He let out a breath and shook his head, without even so much as a glance at the ring. 'I thought you had more sense,' he murmured.

'You never said anything before,' she accused. 'Why now?'

'I thought it was a harmless flirtation, a bit of fun to fill in the time until Terry finally steps up to ask you out. I thought you knew better than to take it seriously.'

'Terry?' She almost spat the name. 'This is about Terry?'

'He's a good young man, and he loves you.'

Peggy put her hands on her hips and let out a long low breath to try to stem the rising swell of fury.

'I don't care if he does love me. I don't love him. Never have and never will. He's a friend and always has been. Nothing more.'

'Then you're a fool.'

She opened her mouth to protest. Her father had never spoken to her this way in all her life, and the shock of it took her breath away.

'Marriage isn't about desire or the romantic love in films or those novels you like so much. It's about friendship and companionship, and making a good life together. The other dies away very quickly, believe me. You need a friend in life, a man you can depend on to be there for you through thick and thin.'

For the first time, she let the possibility of marriage to Terry trickle through her thoughts, struggling to picture it.

Herself as the good doctor's wife in an affluent suburb of Cambridge – quiet evening dinners with well-behaved children who were destined for futures in medicine or law, and the girls brought up to make good marriages. Dinner parties with other doctors and their wives. Then she imagined the two of them in bed at night, polite conversation before dutiful sex, and her guts turned over in revulsion.

'I'm not marrying Terry,' she said. 'I'm going to marry Zack. And I would like your blessing but I'll marry him just the same, with or without it.'

Her father lowered his head with a sigh. 'I don't know what's got into you, Peggy. You used to have more sense.'

'So do I have your blessing or not?'

'Your mother would be very disappointed,' he replied, which didn't answer her question. 'And from now on Zack Eldon is barred from the Queen's Head.'

The pub door swung open with a jangle of the bell and three farmworkers barrelled in, sweaty from their morning's labour and eager for a pint. Peggy turned away and went back to the kitchen, while her father greeted the workers with his customary smile, the one that masked each and every emotion behind it. It was an enviable skill, and she doubted she would ever master it.

Chapter Eleven

1943

The villagers at Sutton Heath had become used to the thunder of planes, pausing in their conversations as the formations of bombers flew overhead and waiting patiently for the noise to diminish before continuing. The British had been flying their night-time raids almost since the war began, and the previous year the Americans had begun their daytime sorties from more distant airfields, their engines a roar in the background and no more than a minor inconvenience.

But the bombers that flew from the new airbase near the village seemed almost close enough to touch as they rumbled over the village and shattered the peace again and again, deafening, a visceral vibration that made the very ground seem to tremble underfoot. They had begun to fly more often now, thundering low across the town as the training stepped up in preparation for the real raids that could not be far away – it was common knowledge that more airmen were arriving all the time from America to man the new airfields springing up all across the east coast of England.

Every time the racket fractured the day, Peggy would stop

whatever she was doing to go to the window and watch them, losing herself in the din and trying to imagine the men aboard, Zack among them. The thought of it played on her mind and disturbed her sleep, filling it with dreams of fire and falling planes, so that she woke each morning groggy and unrefreshed, her thoughts caught in the tail of half-remembered nightmares.

She didn't visit Sylvia. Though she planned to go every day in the hour between the closing of the post office and the opening of the pub, she found she was simply unable to face it. She had imagined her friend's reaction over and over again – the disbelief, the anger, the heartbreak. How could she bring herself to inflict such pain? And, still distraught from the argument with her father, she found she could not quite quash completely the doubts he had roused about her own love affair. She remembered her questions to Zack in the hotel room when he had told her about Jim, and though her heart never wavered in its love and loyalty, a tiny corner of her mind nagged with her father's suspicions. How could she splinter Sylvia's world, when her own was still in such turmoil?

On a quiet evening a few days later Zack came to the pub and Peggy's heart somersaulted in her chest when she saw him at the door – she could feel the heat of the flush of pleasure that coloured her cheeks. But the instinctive rush of delight at the sight of him ceded quickly to dread as her father's figure flashed at the corner of her eye, and she halted abruptly on her journey towards the bar. Carefully, she placed the glasses in her hand on the nearest table, and waited to see what her father would do. In the pause that followed she held her breath, and she saw Zack register her hesitation with the beginnings of a question in his eyes, but he had no time to wonder at its cause.

'You're barred.' Her father's voice was loud from his place behind the bar and the two local farmers who were sitting in the corner looked up from their card game with curiosity, eyes flitting between the landlord and the young American.

Peggy saw the confusion pass across Zack's face, and the smile he had been wearing for her faded, his mouth tightening with tension.

'You're not welcome here any more.'

Peggy set the glass she was holding on the bar and took a step towards him.

'Dad, please,' she heard herself saying. 'It's not his fault.'

Although he had threatened it she had thought it was only in the initial heat of his anger: she had not believed for one moment he would stick to it. Her father swung round to face her and she had never seen such fury in his eyes, jaw working with his anger, lips clamped and hard. Instinctively, she backed away.

'And my daughter ...' – her father gestured to Peggy with a curt nod of his head – '... is also off limits.'

'No!' Peggy found her voice. 'You can't stop me seeing him.'

He swung towards her. 'I can and I will. If I see him sniffing around you again, I'll report him to his commanding officer. It's for your own good, Peggy. I know what he wants from you. I know what he's already had, and he's not going to get any more.'

He stepped out from behind the bar at last. He was a big man, and his bulk seemed to fill the pub.

Peggy moved towards the door, towards Zack, who reached out his arm and drew her into him. His jacket was damp from the night outside but she was aware of his warmth underneath it and she felt safe in the circle of his embrace, as if nothing could ever touch her again.

'I'm going to marry your daughter, sir,' Zack said. 'I don't know what you've been told about me or what you think you know about me, but I would never do anything to hurt her.'

Her father took a step forward and she felt Zack brace against her, the tautened muscles ready and waiting. She flicked a glance up at him and he gave her a small nod of reassurance that did nothing to calm her racing heart. The two men she loved most in the world at each other's throats, because of her.

'You already have hurt her,' her father said. 'You've promised her a world you have no intention of delivering, and in her belief in that promise she's made a fool of herself. What sort of girl spends a weekend with a serviceman she barely knows?' His eyes slid from Zack's face to hers. 'I'll tell you what sort – a girl who's no better than she should be. I'm very disappointed in you, Peggy. I thought you were better than that. Terry's a forgiving man, Peg, but he's not a saint and he won't wait around forever.'

Zack's arm tightened slightly against her and though she could feel his body quivering with tension, when he spoke his voice was calm and even, with no trace of the anger she knew was simmering inside him.

'We're going to get married,' he said again. 'And though we

hoped for your blessing, we'll marry with or without it. I love your daughter and I plan to make a life with her.'

He looked down at Peggy with a small smile.

'Grab your coat. Let's go for a walk.'

With a nod, she slipped out from his clasp, and walked with all the dignity she could muster towards the kitchen at the back of the pub where her coat and hat hung on the hook. She was aware of her father's gaze following her and the hurt in his eyes. She reached for her things with fingers that trembled so hard she could barely control them, shrugged herself into her coat, and forced herself not to run back across the pub to the door, to Zack. When she reached him at last, she did not turn back to look at her father again, but took Zack's hand and stepped out into the cool night of the high street.

Outside, Zack folded her into his arms and she buried her head against his chest, struggling against the sobs she could not hold back. Her whole body shook with emotion, and she held Zack tightly against her, her face pressed against his coat. She was aware of his lips against her hair but he was silent, simply allowing the tears to come, and she was grateful. There was nothing he could say that could comfort her – it seemed her father was a different man from the one she had thought him to be: she had never suspected he could be so unfeeling.

The approaching roar of an army truck in the road dragged her thoughts back to the moment, and she raised her head to look up at Zack. He gave her a small smile and lifted one hand to wipe the tears away from her cheek with gentle fingers. How could it be wrong to love this man; this loving, tender man who was observing her now with sorrow in his eyes at her distress?

'I'm sorry,' she breathed, but her voice came out so choked and ragged, she wasn't sure if he would even understand her.

'He's just trying to protect you,' Zack murmured. 'Because he loves you.'

The truck trundled past them, filling the high street with a stench of fuel, and they stepped apart and watched it go. It was heading to the airbase, she supposed, delivering something or other. Staring after it as it dwindled into the night and the roar of its engine grew fainter, Peggy grasped Zack's hand in her own, holding it fiercely. She had no words to answer him.

When the customary quiet had settled over the village once more, she turned to him. Her breath was still uneven and she was aware of the tears on her face – the night air was cool against them and she raised an automatic hand to wipe them away. Her other hand was still tightly wound in Zack's.

'Shall we walk?' he asked, after a while.

She nodded, not trusting herself to speak. She had almost forgotten they were still standing just outside the pub, her father less than a stone's throw away, and with that realisation, she wanted to go and put distance between them. She was still in shock from the way he had spoken to Zack and the threat he had levelled, and aghast he so firmly believed she would marry Terry. Did he not know her at all? Had all the years she had thought them close taught him nothing about her? Her mother would have understood, she thought. Her mother would have known.

They headed along the high street, following the path of the truck towards the airfield though neither had made a conscious decision, both of them eager simply to move away. It was a cool summer night, soft and damp, and a pale half-moon peered now and then between a shifting veil of cloud, lighting their way. For a while she said nothing, her emotions still roiling in shock. But slowly the turmoil began to lessen with her awareness of Zack's presence at her side, and her unwavering certainty in the rightness of it.

Finally, she turned her head to look at him through the evening gloom as he walked beside her. He was watching the road before his feet, and his face was taut with concentration, brows lightly furrowed. The sight of it lit a small smile inside her and she gave his hand a squeeze.

'I'm so sorry,' she said. 'He had no right to talk to you like that.'

'It's okay,' he replied, with a shrug. 'He cares about you, that's all.'

'It's not okay.' She was adamant. Her dismay at her father's treatment of her had begun to give way to a new fury on Zack's behalf. How dare he talk to him that way, issuing threats? How dare he be so rude to the man she loved?

'It doesn't matter, Peg,' he said softly, and they slowed their steps, standing in the dark in the middle of the lane. The hedgerows on either side rustled with nocturnal life, and behind them she was aware of the low-lying fields stretching away to the horizon, the winter wheat just starting to ripen. They faced each other, fingers still entwined. She loved how they could simply talk with the pressure of their hands together, whole worlds contained within their touch.

'Do you still want to marry me?' he asked, and anyone else might have missed the slight hesitation in the question. But she heard it, and understood.

'Of course I do,' she answered quickly. 'Of course.'

'Even though your dad disapproves?'

'I would still marry you even if the whole world disapproved.'

He grinned. 'Then let's do it. As soon as we can. I just have to get permission …' He trailed off with a shrug as if to say it could still be a while, but it didn't matter. They were getting married, and very soon they would be man and wife. She felt their closeness as a glow that encircled them, a new light that filled every fibre of her being – brilliant and joyful.

She gave him a coy smile as he drew her gently towards him, and all that existed in that moment was the two of them in the early autumn night under the soft light of a half-moon.

Later that evening Zack kissed her goodnight in the street outside the pub, and Peggy was warm with the promise of the wedding to come. She felt as though her limbs were glowing with joy for all the world to see, and the fight with her father was all but forgotten. But when she turned from the man she loved to face the door of the pub, the force of what had been said that night almost felled her like a blow from behind and her footsteps faltered. Zack squeezed her fingers in a gesture of reassurance but it did nothing to help. She did not know what to expect from her father, had no precedent to call upon. Earlier, smaller rows about long-forgotten things had blown over quickly, their differences paling beside the love that connected them. But this was a whole new situation – their first true fight as adults, and she had no idea how he would be when she stepped inside. For the thousandth time, she wished her mother were still alive, and she could call upon the other woman's peacemaking instincts to soothe her father's wrath. Her mother had always known just the right thing to say to calm a situation, and a sudden wash of grief flooded through her. She would have understood, she thought. She would have taken Peggy's part.

'Will you be okay?' Zack asked.

She shrugged. 'I hope so,' she replied, with a small, resigned tilt of her head.

'Do you want me to wait?'

Shaking her head, she fumbled in her bag for the key and slid it into the lock. It turned with the customary hesitation but when she pressed her palm against the door to push it open, it did not give. She shoved it harder in the moment before she realised that her father had bolted it against her.

She turned to Zack in disbelief. 'He's locked me out.'

She rattled the door again in frustration, even though she knew it was futile. The lights inside were all off, she realised, and the place was dark. In his fury, he must have closed up early. Was he listening to her rattling at the door now, imagining her anguish and pleased with himself? She could scarcely believe her father could be so hard-hearted.

'You should go,' she said, turning to Zack. 'I don't want you to get in trouble.'

'I'm not going to leave you in the street, Peg.'

She said nothing but turned from him to begin hammering once more on the door, her hands quickly growing sore with the force. But even as she knocked, she knew that if he was upstairs in the sitting room listening to the wireless he would not hear her, however hard she knocked, and so after a few moments more she gave up the effort, her palms red and aching.

'Is there somewhere you can go?' Zack asked. In the half-dark, she could just see the worry in his eyes, his brow crinkled in the way she was beginning to love so well.

Turning from the door, she sighed and cast her gaze along the high street. The only possible place she could go was to Sylvia's, though her limbs were heavy with reluctance to disturb her friend so late at night. She had called on Sylvia's kindness too often already these last few weeks. But what other choice did she have? She had no other close friends in the village, no one else to turn to. The evening was fast turning into night, and she could hardly sleep on the street.

'Sylvia,' she said, and the two of them walked hand in hand the short distance along the high street to the post office.

Chapter Twelve

1995

Georgia stayed on with her grandmother, despite the whispered arguments on the phone with Scott, who wanted her to come home straight away.

She had spent enough time looking after Nana already.

Nana needed to learn to stand on her own two feet.

Nana could do without her.

Whereas he ...

He complained she didn't love him and though she did her best to reassure him – of course I love you, she told him over and over – gradually she began to wonder if he might in fact be right. She hadn't really missed him all that much through the days they had been apart, she realised. She hadn't missed him at all, in fact, which surprised her. Not so long ago she had been so sure she couldn't live without him she had been willing to forgo marriage and a family just to stay with him. Now, she wasn't even certain she cared if she ever saw him again.

'Are you sure you don't mind being here?' Nana asked a

dozen times a day. 'You must be missing your life in London. What about work?'

'I had some leave owing,' she replied. 'And really, I'm not missing London at all.'

'Not even Scott?'

'No,' she admitted. 'Not even Scott.'

Nana gave her a look that Georgia was not quite sure how to read, and said nothing.

Putting her relationship with Scott from her mind with surprising ease, she focused her thoughts on Zack's history, eager to find out the truth about this young man her grandmother had loved so well, her grandfather. With Nana's approval, she began trying to track down his sister, and she started with a single-page missive addressed to *The Eldon Family, Bliss, Idaho, USA*, in the faint hope that it might find its way to someone who was connected, someone who knew where the family might be now.

On a quiet night that was damp with autumn drizzle, she caught up with a couple of old school friends she hadn't seen for far too long. They met at the Queen's Head, the old-fashioned pub on the village high street that had once been her grandmother's home. It had a big open fireplace, and horse brasses and faded hunting prints hung on wallpapered walls, which gave it a cosy atmosphere. She had always liked it. She remembered Sunday lunches now and then as a child with her grandparents as a special treat, and her first taste of beer as a teenager pretending to be eighteen, even though the barman must have known the truth.

Now, in the light of all Nana had told her, she saw it with

different eyes, trying to imagine the place full of British and American forces, tensions high and tempers flaring. Briefly, she cast a glance across the walls in search of the piano that Peggy and Zack had played on that fateful night, but it had long since disappeared. Casting her mind back, she couldn't recall ever seeing it at all.

Stella and Adie were already at the bar when she arrived, and they greeted her with great hugs of affection. It was wonderful to see them again, too many years since the last time.

'Vodka tonic?' Adie asked, and Georgia laughed. She had forgotten that had been her teenage drink, when the three girls had lied about their age at other pubs where nobody knew them: they had thought themselves so sophisticated. She couldn't remember the last time she had drunk vodka – in her commitment to health and fitness with Scott she rarely had more than the occasional beer: their bodies were temples, he liked to remind her, and alcohol was a poison.

'I'd love one,' she replied.

The barman came through from the back to serve them, and for a moment she stared, taken aback as she recognised Ben Turner, the caterer from Grandpa's funeral. An unexpected flush of pleasure swept across her: though she hadn't given him a single thought since the wake, too absorbed in her grandmother's story to think of much else, now that he was before her again, she remembered that he was really very handsome, with his clear green eyes that crinkled at the edges when he smiled.

Adie ordered their drinks and they took them to a table in the corner. Both women looked well, and happy, Georgia thought, as they caught up on each other's news. Stella was nursing at the local cottage hospital – the only job she had ever wanted to do – and still loving it. Adie had opened her own florist shop in a nearby town and it was flourishing – she had just been hired to do the flowers for a couple of weddings. Georgia recalled with pleasure their shared enjoyment in art class at school – Adie had always hoped to do something creative, and they had talked endlessly about the possibilities: floristry, fashion or jewellery making, – while she, Georgia, had always planned to go to university to study graphic design, eager to develop her talent for drawing. Then Scott had swept her off her feet in her last year at school, and her ambitions had given way to the lure of a love affair and the heady early days of a new life in London.

Now, as she listened to her friends, Georgia felt a pang of envy at their satisfaction. They had followed their dreams, while she was stuck in a job she hated, where the work was tedious and unrewarding.

'I'm thinking of moving back,' she heard herself telling them, though she hadn't planned to. 'I'm sick of London.'

There was a moment of stunned silence as both women stared at her in surprise.

'What about Scott?' Adie asked.

Georgia let out a breath between pursed lips. Dare she put words to the thoughts that had been budding in her mind these last few days? Thoughts that time away from him had given room to take root. She swallowed.

'I'm going to leave him,' she said, and let out a laugh that was half relief and half terror.

'You've been with him forever,' Stella said. 'Since school.'

'I know,' she replied, 'and we've had a lot of fun together. He's not a bad person or anything but I just …' she trailed off.

How could she explain it to them when she could hardly understand it herself? She tried again. 'I feel like I've lost who I am a bit – my life always takes second place to his. And he doesn't want children. Doesn't want to get married.'

Her friends exchanged a look that made Georgia narrow her eyes.

'What?' she demanded. 'What is it?'

Adie turned to her quickly. 'I'm pleased for you,' she said. 'It's very brave.'

'I haven't even spoken to Nana about it yet. I'll need to stay with her for a while, and find a job, which could be hard.'

'Can you cook?' Ben's voice cut in to their conversation. He must have been listening from his place at the bar where he was idly wiping down the counters and checking the pumps. All three women turned towards him in startlement.

'Yes,' Georgia replied. 'I can cook.' She was almost insulted. 'Why do you ask?'

He stepped away from the bar and came towards them, but his gaze was directed only at Georgia. She felt herself blush under the intensity of his attention, his green eyes trained on her face.

'You can have a job here if you like,' he said. 'Five mornings a week: soup, pies, and doorstop sandwiches. Nothing too demanding. I've been doing it myself the last few months, but some help would be very welcome.'

She hesitated.

'Just casual,' he went on. 'Cash in hand. If you don't like it you don't have to stay. But it could tide you over for a bit, and it would definitely help me out.' He shrugged and wiped down a neighbouring table with the cloth that was in his hand, as if to say it was neither here nor there to him.

She looked at her friends.

Adie said, 'Why not? You've nothing to lose,' and Stella nodded in enthusiastic agreement.

'Well ...'

Though she understood the universe was holding out a hand to help her bridge the step away from London, she wasn't quite sure what to say. She had only made the decision to leave London that very night, and a part of her was reluctant to accept, afraid that it would set the decision in stone. After all, she had yet to break up with Scott and the thought of it weighed like lead in her guts. It was going to be awful and even now, with the decision all but made, a little voice in her head whispered that she would be a fool to leave him.

'She'll take it.' Adie accepted the offer for her, and Georgia laughed.

'Great!' Ben said, and turned again to face them. 'Can you start on Monday?'

'I suppose I could.' She found her voice at last, still in shock at the sudden turn she had just taken in her life, a new beginning. 'Though I do still have a life in London to wrap up.'

'And a boyfriend to dump,' Stella supplied, with her usual forthright manner.

'Yes,' Georgia agreed with a rueful laugh. 'And a boyfriend to dump.'

Then she went to the bar and asked Ben Turner for another vodka tonic.

Nana was delighted when Georgia told her the news over breakfast the next morning.

'Are you sure you don't mind me staying? It might be for a while.'

'I'd love to have you here,' Nana said. 'Besides, I'm just overjoyed you've seen the light about Scott at last. All these years I've watched the wonderful Georgia I knew fade into a shadow of the person she used to be. Perhaps you could go back and study. Do you still draw?'

'Now and then,' Georgia replied. 'But not as often as I'd like. We're always doing stuff – hiking or training for hiking, or just some new exercise regime that takes up all our time.' She gave her grandmother a rueful shrug.

'Well, you do look very healthy,' Nana admitted. 'So I suppose all that fitness training has been good for something, but you need more than that. You need food for your soul. An outlet for your imagination. You were always so creative as a child – it almost broke my heart when you decided not to go to art school after all.'

'You never said anything!'

'Of course not! You were in love, and you would have taken absolutely no notice of me at all.'

Georgia swallowed and said nothing. She was perfectly right, of course. She had been besotted by Scott and would have heard no words against him, eager and willing to throw her life at his feet. A better man, she realised now, would have encouraged her to follow her dreams. They could have made it work somehow, if he had been willing, but his whole world revolved around his own ambition and she had been reduced to playing second fiddle. How could she have been so blind?

'I'm going back to London on the afternoon train to …' She stopped, eyes grazing the walls as she searched for the right way to express it. '… to finish things with Scott.'

The words seemed to belong to someone else, as if such a thing might be possible for another person, but not for her. She recalled Stella's words – *a boyfriend to dump* – and her guts lurched at the thought of it. Her friend had made it sound so easy, and here, far away in a different life, it didn't seem so hard to embrace her freedom. But she knew that confronting Scott would be one of the most difficult things she had ever done. In London was the life they had made together, their home, and resisting his entreaties face-to-face would take every ounce of her resolve. Even now, she still wondered if she had the will to carry through.

'This time tomorrow it will be over,' Nana said, laying a reassuring hand on her granddaughter's forearm. Her touch was gentle and light, and Georgia was suffused with the familiar sense of safety her grandmother had given her ever since she could remember. Looking up, she met Nana's gaze, so full of love, and her own eyes began to well with tears.

Chapter Thirteen

1995

The train journey seemed to take no time at all and far before she was ready Georgia found herself on the platform at Liverpool Street, walking towards the ticket barrier along with all the other passengers.

All the way from Sutton Heath she had gazed out of the window and watched the countryside flitter past, imagining all the lives that were being lived in the houses that she saw, and the doubts that played in her head had refused to be silenced. Scott had been her first boyfriend, her only lover. She had grown from schoolgirl to woman at his side. Everything she had ever done as an adult she had done with him. Every journey, every holiday, every sport and activity – her whole life centred on his company. All her decisions until today had been filtered through him. What would he think of it? What would he prefer? Would he approve? It was almost impossible to imagine her life without him, and leaving him seemed to be an almost unfathomable step away from the life she had been living for so many years, a great leap of faith into the unknown.

But in truth, she was itching to start again and be her own person. A new life. A new job. The possibility of art school beckoning again. The future was waiting, she told herself, an adventure to be lived, and Scott had no part to play in it.

On the other side of the ticket gate she found a payphone and paused beside it, taking her time to dig out some change from her purse, dredging deep for the courage to call. Her heart was pounding in her chest, her mouth dry and chalky, and her nervousness infuriated her. She was leaving a man she no longer loved – it should be a cause for celebration, not anxiety. But however hard she tried to rationalise, her body refused to listen.

Twice, she picked up the receiver and put it down again. Then, finally, with a long breath and a little lift of her shoulders, she snatched it up and punched his office number onto the keypad. The line took a moment to connect then rang three, four, five times, and when he answered at last, she spoke quickly, delivering the lines she had rehearsed on the train.

He wasn't remotely surprised to hear she was in London – he had been expecting her home for days. But when she suggested they go out that night for dinner somewhere because they needed to talk, a sudden tension pulsed through the phone line.

'It's Wednesday. I'm going to the gym after work,' he said. 'Can't it wait?'

'No,' she said. 'It can't.'

There was a silence.

'I'll meet you at Fernando's. Seven o'clock?'

He sighed, irritated, but he must have heard the tone of

decision in her voice because he offered no more argument. She allowed herself a small smile of relief.

'All right,' he said. 'I'll see you there.' Then he hung up and the line went dead.

Her heart was still racing. But in the few words of that phone conversation, she had understood there was no turning back. She could no longer live her life to please him – she wanted to live in Sutton Heath and drink vodka tonic with her friends. She wanted to go to art school and rediscover the joy that art once had given her. Long lazy Sundays and walks in the countryside. Days at the Queen's Head alongside Ben Turner.

And the trail of Zack Eldon's history that beckoned.

Scott was late to the restaurant, and while she was waiting Georgia took out the book she had been reading on the train, a Graham Greene novel that Nana had recommended. It was a sad and poignant love story set during the war, and she knew why her grandmother loved it – it must have evoked all manner of memories and heartache. Not for the first time, Georgia wondered how people had ever managed to live through such difficult times – the hardship and loss were almost beyond her ability to comprehend.

When, finally, Scott arrived, she could see from the set of his jaw and the angle of his body that he was angry with her – it was a familiar expression, his mouth drawn into a thin tight line, his forehead creased into a furrow. She gave a small inward sigh. They had been apart for days and yet apparently the gym was still more important than she was. With a pang of regret, she realised it had always been the same, even in the early days when she had thought they existed solely for each other.

Offering her no kiss of greeting and barely even a smile of hello, Scott slid into the seat across from her. Her resolution hardened.

'Hi,' she said, with a small, encouraging smile that was more for her own sake than for his. 'I'm back.'

'Finally,' he replied.

Then, perhaps realising that he was being unreasonable, he gave her the smile that had made her fall in love with him in the first place. Even now it was hard to resist – his whole face boyish and charming in its light. She could quite understand why he was so successful in his chosen profession of marketing – who could fail to fall under the spell of such charisma? She braced herself, hardening her heart against the temptation it offered. She had made a decision. She had accepted a new job. There was no going back.

'Shall we order?'

Fernando's was a regular haunt, and they had no need to study the menu. They would share the usual capricciosa pizza with a green salad and garlic bread. It was about as unhealthy as Scott ever allowed himself to eat, his diet a strict regime of fresh vegetables and protein, one coffee a day. Georgia toyed with having a beer but decided against it: she wanted a clear head and sometimes even a single drink could cloud her thinking.

When the waiter had left, Scott turned the full light of his attention on to her, and a flurry of nerves spiralled through her insides as all the words she had rehearsed over the last few hours utterly deserted her. She took a sip of water and straightened her cutlery. Her mouth was dry, and she was aware of the rapid patter of her heart. Briefly, she wondered if she had the strength to end it after all.

'Good to be back?' he asked. He was more relaxed again now, having put aside his initial irritation. The restaurant was warm and comfortable, and the aroma of Italian food was beguiling. It was a familiar setting and she had chosen it deliberately.

'Kind of,' she replied.

He raised a quizzical eyebrow.

'I'm not staying,' she blurted. It was not how she had planned to tell him at all but in the end those were the words that came out of her mouth.

'What do you mean?'

She could see the incomprehension in his face, the struggle to make sense of what she had said.

'I mean that I'm moving back to Sutton Heath,' she said, as gently as she could. 'I'm leaving you.'

She watched him closely, observing the range of emotions that flickered through his eyes. Shock and disbelief, transmuting swiftly to hurt and anger.

'But why?' he managed to say.

She took a deep breath, and the words she had prepared finally appeared in her mind.

'Because we're not good for each other any more,' she said. 'Because I don't want to live in London and work for an insurance company. I want more free time to draw and paint and study. I don't want to spend my life at the gym, and I don't want to put my own dreams aside to support you in yours any more.'

He stared, and she could not remember another time she had ever seen him speechless. Now that she had finally said the words, what followed came more easily. But her heart was still hammering – it wasn't over yet.

'I want a family. I want a man who's willing to plan a future with me, with children, and that's not what you want. Your career is everything to you and you need a partner who is happy with that. I'm not. Not any more. I want more than you can give me, and it's over.'

'Did your grandmother put you up to this?' he breathed, low and soft, so that she barely heard him over the muted hubbub of the restaurant. 'She's always disliked me.'

'No, of course she didn't.' The accusation astonished her, and her defence of Nana was immediate. 'But the time away has given me some space to think about what I want from my life, space that didn't get distracted by your smile.' She gave him a small smile of her own that he didn't return. 'I'm sorry, Scott. I truly am.'

He said nothing but sat back in his chair, putting distance between them. She watched him as his gaze wandered across the restaurant, looking everywhere but at her, and she wondered what he would do. She knew for sure that he would be too proud to beg her to stay, but she was wary of his anger, conscious he might just turn nasty. There was a spiteful side to him that he let out only rarely, but the knowledge of it meant she had spent all the years they had been together treading with care and it was one of the reasons she had chosen to meet him in Fernando's. At last, he brought his eyes back to her and leaned forward on his forearms so that he was quite close to her, his gaze so hard it was like being skewered on a pin.

'You ungrateful bitch,' he snarled. 'After all I've done for you.'

She recoiled at the insult, taken aback in spite of all she knew of him, and felt the blood flood her face, heat in her limbs. Adrenaline coursed through her veins and she could think of nothing at all to say in her own defence.

'I gave you everything,' he said. 'I supported you, encouraged you, made you fit and strong and healthy ... and you throw it back in my face.'

'And I'm grateful.' She found her voice at last. 'I don't regret the years we've had together but I'm not in love with you any more.'

He was silent then, no reply to her bald statement of the truth.

'I just need to collect my stuff,' she said, 'and then I'll be gone. I've arranged for a van to come in the morning for the bigger things.' Her books and pictures. Some of the linen. Her favourite frying pan. An ornament or two. The cheese plant. But really, there wasn't much in the flat of hers at all. It was all his – her life, her tastes, her possessions were just an afterthought in the life they had shared. Scott's life, she understood now, that she had fitted into.

He lifted a hand to his face and rubbed at his chin, eyes searching the restaurant once more for some answer he would never find.

'I'm sorry,' she said again. And she meant it. However much she wanted to begin again, it was still hard to say goodbye to the life she had known with him. Tears began to well behind her eyes, brimming with sorrow and regret. She still couldn't quite believe she had actually ended it.

All Scott's energy seemed to wash out of him in a rush, and he looked weary suddenly, tired of life. The boyish charm of before had deserted him, and she could no longer see in him the man she had loved. Regret sidled into relief that it was done, and she wondered why she had waited so long to do it.

'Go and get your things,' he said, without looking at her. 'Leave the keys. I'll stay at Mike's tonight.'

The waiter brought the pizza and the garlic bread and arranged them with care on the table. He paused to smile at them both, waiting for the customary conversation – they had been regulars at this place for years. But he must have sensed the tension because after only a moment's hesitation, he backed quickly away. Georgia slid her gaze across the meal. Earlier, she had been hungry and looking forward to the pizza, but she couldn't face so much as a single bite now.

As they sat in awkward silence with the meal between them, she wished things had worked out differently, and for the length of a heartbeat she was tempted to change her mind and put things back to how they had been before, safe and unfrightening, another attempt to make it work. But the thought receded as quickly as it arose – in her core, she knew she had made the right decision.

She got to her feet and tucked her handbag over her shoulder, then stepped out from the table.

'I'm sorry, Scott,' she said again.

Then, with a light touch of her fingers to his shoulder as she passed by him, she walked out of the restaurant and out of his life forever.

Chapter Fourteen

1943

The early morning was overcast and a damp mist hung over the village when Peggy stepped out of the post office and into the high street. Lifting a glance to the glowering clouds that sailed dark and low overhead with their promise of more rain, she drew her coat tightly around her. Then she turned back to give her friend a smile of thanks and farewell.

'Let me know what happens,' Sylvia called after her and, with a nod, Peggy turned and bent her footsteps towards the pub.

She had spent a sleepless, teary night on Sylvia's sofa after Zack had left them to return to the base, and her friend had been aghast with shock and disbelief when Peggy told her what had happened.

'Of course you can stay.' She had beckoned her friend inside, and held her tightly. 'Of course.'

Now, as she trudged the short distance along the street she was still reeling with shock and fatigue, devastated that her father would lock his doors against her. Dread dragged at her insides and seemed to add weight to her feet so that it felt as though she were wading through water, each step an effort almost too hard to make. She had no idea what reception awaited her, if he would even take her back.

Outside the pub she halted, searching deep inside herself to find her courage before she tried the door again, turning the handle with tentative fingers. But it swung easily open under her touch, unlocked as it always was at this time, ready for deliveries. She slid inside, her heart drumming in her chest and her breathing quick. She couldn't recall ever being so afraid of her father and, though she was certain of her rightness, a thick thread of guilt trickled through her – the instinctive reaction of a child who is in trouble.

'Hello?' she called, and her voice came out in an uncertain waver. There was no answer and she called again, more confidently this time, forcing her tone to give away nothing of the fear that trembled behind it. 'Dad?'

Her father's figure appeared through the door that led out behind the bar, and they stood for a moment, the whole width of the pub between them. He rested his hands on the counter and watched her, waiting for her to say something – an apology, she supposed. He looked weary, she thought, lines etched deep in his forehead, skin pale. Perhaps he too had suffered a sleepless night.

'Hello, Dad,' she said. Her tone was neutral.

He gave her a small nod but kept his eyes away from hers, and there was a silence that was thick enough to cut with a knife, neither of them knowing what to say. For three long breaths she wondered if they were going to talk about it at all or if they were going to do the British thing and act as though nothing had happened. Drained of emotion and unutterably weary, it was tempting. But there were things that needed to be said and they must live together somehow, so though she was sure it wasn't the best way to start the conversation, she knew she had to say something.

'Why did you lock me out last night?'

He hesitated and she waited, observing him as his eyes swept the length of the bar before him, muscle twitching in his jaw before finally he stood up straight and faced her across the bar.

He said, 'You disrespected me. In front of customers. I was angry.' He stopped. 'I'm *still* angry.'

'Where did you expect me to go?'

'I've given you everything,' he replied, which didn't answer her question. 'Your whole life you've wanted for nothing.'

'You turned me out on the street, Dad.'

He said nothing but looked at her as though she were a stranger, and she thought again that despite all the years of their closeness, they really didn't know each other at all.

'I'm going to marry Zack,' she said then, because she could think of nothing else to say, and in the end, this was the cause of the rift. 'I'm sure Terry has told you lots of terrible things about Americans, and probably some of them are true.' She thought of Jim and Sylvia, who had yet to learn the truth. 'There are good and bad people everywhere – of course there are – but it's not fair to judge Zack on the strength of that.'

Her words seemed to goad her father into speech. 'I'm not judging him on what Terry told me. I'm judging him on the fact he seduced you into a secret dirty weekend away in London. That's not the action of an honourable man, and that's a fact.'

'Zack wanted to ask your permission,' she answered, 'but *I* said no, because I thought you'd refuse.'

'And you were right. I would've.'

'I'm not a child any more, Dad. I'm twenty-four years old—'

'While you're under my roof you'll live by my rules,' her father interrupted.

There was a pause. From outside, they heard a man's voice calling out to someone in the high street, shattering the silence that hung across the pub.

'So where does that leave us?' she asked, and her heart was tight with anxiety as though a great hand were squeezing it.

He hesitated, and she barely dared to breathe. The silence lingered. The man outside was still shouting to someone across the street in a querulous tone, but his words went unheard.

'We're going to get married, Dad,' she heard herself saying in the hush, and though she spoke in barely more than a whisper, her voice sounded loud in the breathless quiet of the pub. Her fury at his rudeness to Zack began to crumble with the desire to win his consent. 'We're going to get married.'

He took in a great breath and his shoulders heaved. He said nothing, and she began to sense a weakening in his resolve to oppose her.

'Dad?' She moved across the pub floor to face him across the bar, no more than a yard away. He was standing with his arms crossed, looking past her shoulder at some unknown thing beyond the walls of the pub. 'I love Zack, and he's a good man. Please understand. I've never loved Terry. I never will. And I know you think that being a doctor's wife would be a good life and perhaps it would, but that's not enough for me. Zack and I are in love – I can't imagine my life without him. You and Mum married because you loved each other –

you've told me so a hundred times.' She paused and, when he did not reply, she went on. 'What would you have done if Gramps had said no?'

His eyes remained steadfastly away from her, still fixed on a spot beyond her shoulder. But she saw the flicker of emotion that passed across his features: she had touched a nerve.

'Dad?'

Finally, he brought his gaze to rest on her face, and he observed her as though seeing her for the first time, trying to read what he saw there. She waited, aware of the tears that were close behind her eyes and the rapid patter of her pulse. Would he see her desperation? Would his love for her win whatever battle was waging inside of him? Although she would marry Zack whatever her father said, it would all but break her heart if he refused to give them his blessing.

He sighed. 'You are so very like your mother.'

She gave him a half-smile then and wiped at her eyes with impatient fingers, unable to hold back the tears any longer. 'Oh, Dad.'

He returned the smile with a small shake of his head, and she could see the glisten of his own tears in the corners of his eyes. Then she opened the hatchway in the bar and ducked through so that she was standing right beside him behind the bar, as they had stood so many times before.

'Is he really going to marry you?'

She nodded.

'And then what? How will you be together?'

'As best we can,' she murmured, 'until the war's over.'

'And then?'

'I don't know.' She shrugged. They had talked about the

possibility of New York but those kind of decisions seemed to belong in a far-off and mythical future after the war. Right now, it was almost impossible to believe that such a time would ever actually come: a world at peace seemed to be no more than a distant memory, an impossible dream. 'We'll cross that bridge when we get to it.'

'Well …' he began, and she balled her fists to contain her impatience. '… I suppose that if you're set on it there's not much I can do to stop you, is there?'

'So we have your blessing?' Her heart skipped a beat, hope kindling.

He let out a breath. 'Yes, I suppose you do.' His answer was drawn out and reluctant, but she didn't care, and flung herself into his arms as she used to do as a child. The tears came in earnest then and there was nothing she could do to stop them.

When the pub closed after lunch and she had finished cleaning up, she scrawled a hurried note to Zack to give him the news, and walked with it out to the airbase. It was a cool afternoon and the air was soft and damp with a drizzle that settled in her hair and on her shoulders. Puddles had filled the potholes in the road under her feet and she skirted round them, but she barely noticed either the rain or the distance she had to walk – she was floating on air.

She left the letter with the sentry, who promised to see it delivered, and turned back to wander slowly home with a small smile playing at the corners of her mouth. But by the time she reached the village, the drizzle had hardened into a more persistent rain that found its way under her collar and into her shoes, and she approached the pub eagerly, warmth and dry clothes beckoning. Then the little red sign that hung above the post office further down the road caught at the edge of her vision and she slowed her steps with a sigh.

Sylvia was a good friend. She had taken Peggy in late last night without a word of complaint, consoling her with tea and a comforting shoulder to cry on. They had always been there for each other, right from their earliest days at school. A ripple of guilt sidled through her, taking the edge off her own sense of joy. Sylvia needed to know the truth, and it was unfair of Peggy not to tell her. Letting out a long sigh of resignation and tilting her shoulders to set herself to the task, she trudged past the pub and along the street towards the post office.

The door opened with a tinkle of the bell, and Sylvia's mother looked up from her place behind the counter where she was counting out stamps. The shop was empty of customers and her friend was nowhere to be seen.

'Hello, love.' Mrs Simpson greeted her. 'Did it go all right with your dad?'

'I think so,' she replied. Though he seemed to have forgiven her she was aware that she had hurt him, and that Zack had yet to earn his trust. It would be a while, she guessed, before the wounds entirely healed. 'Fingers crossed.'

'I'm glad to hear it,' Mrs Simpson said. 'But if not, you know you've always got a place to stay here. Might just be the sofa, but it's a roof at least.'

Peggy felt tears of gratitude well behind her eyes and she sniffed them down.

'Thank you,' she managed to murmur. 'That's very kind.'

'Sylvia's upstairs. It's been a quiet afternoon, so there was no need for us both down here. Go on up, she'll be pleased to see you.'

'Thank you,' Peggy said again, and batted away the thought that she would not be so pleased when she heard what Peggy had to say.

She found her friend making pastry in the kitchen, hands coated with dough and a streak of flour across one cheek. Sylvia looked up quickly from her work.

'What happened?'

'Dad relented,' she said, going to the stove to fetch the kettle. She was as at home in this kitchen as her own at the pub. 'Terry had been spinning him awful tales about Americans, and then he was just upset about me going to London. Hard for him to lose his little girl to another man, I suppose. I've been his whole world for so long.'

Sylvia finished patting the ball of pastry into shape and set the bowl to one side. Then she went to the sink to wash her hands.

'You're really getting married?' She turned to Peggy with a grin. 'You lucky thing! I keep waiting for Jim to propose, but he's starting to get a bit testy if I mention after the war …'

Peggy turned from the stove and let out a long breath, nerves rippling through her. She knew she had to say it, but she was about to break her friend's heart and her whole body pulsed with reluctance.

'He isn't going to ask you, Syl,' she managed to whisper.

Her friend's head jerked up and she grew very still. The silence in the kitchen seemed to deepen.

'What do you mean?' Sylvia replied, her voice no more

than a murmur. Her eyes were wide, her face pale, as though she already suspected the truth. 'What do you mean?'

Peggy swallowed. 'He's already married. He's got two kids.'

Sylvia shook her head and the tip of her tongue slid over her lips as she looked away, searching for a different answer somewhere across the kitchen floor. 'That's a lie.'

'He was showing photos to the guys in the mess. His wife had sent them – pictures from his daughter's birthday party …' She trailed off, heart turning in pity for her friend, whose face seemed to crumple. 'I'm so sorry, Syl. I didn't want to tell you but I had to.'

Sylvia felt for the chair back with her hand and lowered herself into the seat. Her eyes seemed to gaze at nothing as she fought to make sense of the words she had just heard. She had allowed herself to fall in love with a man who was a liar and a cheat, and her whole world had just been shattered. Peggy watched the struggle and the gradual acceptance of the truth – fitting the facts together, she guessed, and finding understanding.

'The bastard!' she said finally, and the words were barely more than a whisper.

Peggy finished making the tea and set the pot and cups on the table. They sat in silence as they waited for it to brew; Peggy could think of nothing else to say. She raised her head to look out of the little window above the sink. The rain was falling harder now, spattering against the glass. Neither of them spoke, and Sylvia's gaze rested on some point far beyond the window, her face a mask.

She took a mouthful of tea. It was weak and tasteless, the week's ration running low, but it was comforting nonetheless, a familiar ritual. She observed her friend, who was still silent with shock and anger. Peggy had expected more tears – Sylvia had always been the emotional one of the two of them, with a hot-headed streak that had led them into trouble more than once.

Finally, Sylvia put her cup back in its saucer and looked at Peggy with a steady gaze across the table. Her eyes were still quite dry but there was an awful stillness about her that pricked a sense of fear in Peggy.

'I should have known,' she whispered.

'How could you have known?'

'Because I always pick the bad ones ...' Her pretty lips clamped tight, and Peggy could see the struggle to keep the tears from coming.

'That isn't true,' she said.

Sylvia let out a harsh laugh. 'Yes it is. You're very sweet to say so Peg, but you know I do.'

'Oh Syl.'

'But I really thought Jim was different. He's so kind and generous. So thoughtful ...' She shook her head in bafflement that she had allowed herself to believe him.

'I was naming our children, designing my wedding dress, and all this time, it was just a lie.'

She lost the fight against the tears and lowered her face into her hands. 'How could I be so stupid?'

Peggy said nothing – what answer could she possibly give? Instead, she reached her hand across the table and squeezed her friend's fingers with her own. Sylvia's shoulders heaved and she began to weep in earnest, her heart breaking, her sobs the only sound in the silent kitchen as the rain beat hard against the window.

. . .

On Saturday night, the pub was busy with locals and airmen, voices raised in a hubbub of sound. Peggy wove between the tables collecting empties as her father served the endless queue for drinks at the bar. Zack sat with Freddie near the piano and now and then she paused in her work to be with them for a moment or two, warming herself in the glow of his attention. She knew that his eyes followed her movements as she went to and fro across the pub and it made the work seem light.

The crowd was finally beginning to dwindle, customers heading out into the last of the evening light. Their voices carried from the street as they milled and chatted, saying their goodbyes, and Peggy and her father were just starting to clean up, collecting the empties, when the door opened abruptly and a lone airman barrelled in. Peggy looked up in surprise.

It took her only a moment to realise it was Jim, although he was barely recognisable as the laughing young man she had seen so often with her friend. His face was flushed with rage, his jaw set tight. At his sides, his hands were balled into fists. She cast a warning look towards Zack but he had already seen. She watched him drain off the last of his beer and move the glass to one side.

'Did you tell her?' Jim took a couple of steps deeper into the pub towards Zack and Freddie.

The last remaining drinkers stopped their conversations to watch as the harsh shout rang out across the murmur.

'I told her.' Peggy stepped forward into his path. 'She had a right to know.'

The airman looked her over, and hesitated.

'It's only the truth, after all,' she said. And though she was aware of the rapid throb of her heartbeat and the dryness of her mouth there was no trace of fear in her voice, her tone calm and steady.

Her father came out from behind the bar.

'You need to leave, my friend,' he said softly. 'I don't want trouble in my pub.'

Jim stared for a moment as though he hadn't understood, before his eyes began to track across the pub – Peggy, Zack, and all the other drinkers, watching him. He was breathing hard. Then all the fight seemed to drain out of him in a wave and with a resigned shake of his head he turned abruptly and left, slamming the door behind him.

Peggy's father turned to her. 'What was that about? That was Sylvia's fellow, wasn't it?'

She took a deep breath and passed her tongue across her lips. Her pulse was still racing from the confrontation as she looked up at him, waiting for an answer.

'He's married,' she made herself say, and instinctively felt for the little ruby on her hand, turning the ring lightly between her fingers. It had become a habit since she had begun to wear it openly, the ring like a talisman she touched for luck.

Her father said nothing, but merely turned away and went back to his place behind the bar, collecting an empty mug from one of the tables on his way. Peggy looked across to Zack, who shrugged. But she guessed the fight would flare again, at the airbase perhaps, or on the road from the village. She went to sit with him for a moment, the first chance they'd had to exchange more than a few words all evening.

'Will it be all right?' she asked. 'Will he pick a fight with you later?'

'Maybe.' Zack seemed unconcerned. 'But he's on his own. No one's going to defend that kind of behaviour.'

Later, when they were alone together, she would tell him the whole story but for now she simply nodded her agreement. Then, with a glance across her shoulder she saw that the last customers were leaving.

'I've got to get back to work.'

'And we have to get back to the base.' Freddie nudged his friend's arm with his elbow.

She stood and watched them go – the two young airmen stepping out into the starless dark of the night, the cloud cover low and heavy. Warmth flickered through every part of her, a sense of rightness, and the near-fight with Jim was already forgotten.

Chapter Fifteen

1943

Autumn seemed to slide into winter overnight and the rainstorms swept the changing leaves from the trees to form a soft moist carpet, slippery underfoot. A new damp chill hung in the air that seeped under their clothes, a promise of the colder days to come. And still their permission to get married had not come through.

'Military wheels turn slowly,' Zack said. 'It's not a priority.'

She understood but even so, her heart ached with longing to be Zack's wife and to have her father's blessing. Because in spite of their truce, she knew he wouldn't truly be content until there was a wedding.

Zack was on an overnight pass and they were walking together through the pretty Cambridge streets in the soft afternoon. Taking their time to wander arm in arm, they were chatting about this and that – the easy unending chit-chat they had shared since the very first time they met, conversation that could veer in a moment from a spirited debate about politics or books to the idle discussion of the things in the windows of the shops that they passed or the best kind of tea.

They had walked as far as the river and they stopped now, watching two children on the path with a small dog that was chasing the ducks. Zack turned to her.

'Is Sylvia okay?'

'No, not really,' she replied. 'She's heartbroken. She thought he was the one. She really did.'

Zack shook his head in silent pity. 'He's not the only guy to string a girl along like that. I'm ashamed to say your dad was right to have his doubts about us Yanks.'

She said nothing. Her father had been silent when she told him she was going overnight to Cambridge, but she had seen the glint of disapproval in his eyes before he turned and walked away from her. She hadn't mentioned it to Zack. A sudden breeze caught at the rain on the overhanging trees, and the droplets were cold against her hair. Peggy shivered and nestled closer into Zack's embrace.

'Let's not talk about it,' she said, 'not now.' She didn't want to think about her friend's unhappiness and the man who had caused it. Not now, when she was here with Zack and her own life was perfect. 'Shall we walk on?'

He nodded and they sauntered on as the rain clouds darkened overhead, weaving through the streets on a winding route back to their hotel not far from the city centre. They reached it just as the first raindrops began to fall, and exchanged a look of relief as they hurried up the marble steps to the door. It was grander than any place she had ever stayed before, and she was eager to see inside.

'One of the guys recommended it,' Zack told her, as she stood by the polished oak front desk, looking around the lobby. Tall windows with damask curtains let in the light, and her heels clicked on the immaculate black and white tiles underfoot. She had to remind herself that not so far away the war was raging. 'Nice, huh?'

'Very,' she agreed.

'Nothing but the best for the future Mrs Eldon.'

'That's me,' she replied, with another smile. The name sent a warm flush through her, cheeks burning with pleasure, and she tightened her grip on Zack's hand. It would take some getting used to, she thought, but she liked it.

The elderly clerk at the reception desk was polite, and if he doubted their marital status he said nothing: she supposed it was the kind of hotel where guests were not to be judged. A memory of the hotel in London and the clerk's look of disdain flickered through her thoughts, recalling the way he had tried to make her feel ashamed. She ushered it away – she felt no remorse at all for loving Zack, nor for spending the night with him at the hotel. In a world at war and so full of hate, how could it be a crime to love someone? Absently she twisted the ring on her finger while Zack filled out the paperwork. Then he was leading her by the hand up the stairs towards their room.

In the corridor they halted outside their door, and Zack slid the key into the lock. It turned with a satisfying clunk and he pushed it open. Then, turning to her again with a grin that brightened his whole face, he swept her off her feet in his arms and carried her into the room as though she were his bride, slamming the door shut behind them with his foot. Taken by surprise, she let out a laugh, but she held on to him tightly and all the nerves of before evaporated in the safety of his clasp. She had never before felt so at ease, so loved, so right.

Pretending to stagger under her weight, he collapsed with

her onto the bed, making her laugh again. Then they were lying together on top of the covers and as he looked down into her eyes, the laughter gave way to some other emotion she was not sure she could even name.

His mouth was very close to her face and she could feel the warmth of his breath on her cheek. She was aware of every part of her body that was touching his, his chest against her breasts, his leg wrapped around hers. His lips brushed her forehead and she felt her breath lift in her chest. Zack's breathing quickened too as his mouth touched her eyelids, her nose, her cheek. She closed her eyes to focus on the feeling and tilted her head away when his lips sought out the line of her jaw and the delicate skin of her neck.

She had not expected they would come to this so soon. She had thought there would be dinner and a couple of drinks, and then bed. But it was four o'clock in the afternoon, broad daylight, and they were already here.

'Are you okay?' he asked.

She snapped open her eyes.

'Yes!' she answered straight away, wondering why he would ask. 'Of course. Why wouldn't I be?'

'We were supposed to be married by now.'

'It's fine. It doesn't matter, really it doesn't.'

'Are you sure? With your dad and everything ...'

She brushed the backs of her fingers across his cheek, the stubble rough against her skin. She could see the doubt in his eyes, and the worry that her father's disapproval might yet prove their undoing. She looked up at him and smiled.

'There is nowhere else in the world I'd rather be than here with you, married or not. Life is perfect. I wouldn't change a single thing.'

Footsteps sounded in the corridor outside the door and instinctively they held their breath, as though someone might burst through the door and tell them to stop. Then as the steps diminished along the passage, Zack lowered his head to hers and kissed her.

With his kiss, any last remaining doubts receded into the afternoon around them. His hand sought out her breast through the thin cotton of her dress. Then, dragging at the buttons, he felt for the skin underneath, finding his way beneath her slip and her brassiere, and she shivered with his touch. She was conscious of the weight of his body against hers, his warmth and hardness, and she began to fumble for his belt, fingers searching for the clasp. He let out a low moan as her hand freed him from his pants and then, in one agile move, he shifted his body over hers and entered her. Her back arched in pleasure and she wrapped her legs around his hips, drawing him deeper inside her as they moved together in flawless harmony. A perfect duet, she thought, a song that would never end.

Afterwards, they lay wrapped in each other on top of the covers, growing cool with the fading afternoon, but neither of them wanted to move and break the perfection of the moment. She closed her eyes and let herself drift in the sweetness of the aftermath.

When she opened them again, the rain had stopped and the light had changed in the room. A long shadow fell through the window, dust motes sparkling in the late afternoon sunlight. Zack was lying beside her on his side, watching her, and she realised she must have slept for a while.

'How long was I asleep?' she asked.

'Not long,' he answered. 'You're beautiful when you're sleeping,' he said. 'So peaceful.'

She laughed. 'And the rest of the time?'

'Still beautiful. But rarely peaceful.'

She said nothing but turned on her side to face him. He reached a hand to touch her face and she closed her eyes, nuzzling her cheek against his palm like a cat. Then he bent to kiss her and made love to her again.

Finally, hunger drove them from their bed and, though the hotel had its own highly recommended restaurant, they wanted to walk together through the city again. The rain had cleared and left in its wake a soft cool damp, the clouds rimmed with the last light of the dying day as the dark began to creep across the sky.

They ate dinner at a small restaurant they came upon by chance in a side street. It was quiet, and a young girl was playing the piano in the corner – soft American jazz that was perfect for their mood.

'After the war,' she said, 'shall we live in New York?'

'We can live wherever you want to,' he said. 'As long as there are bars and hotels where I can play music.'

'I think I'd like to try New York,' she said. 'It sounds exciting. But London would be nearer to Dad.'

In the sleepless hours of nights alone and during idle moments of the day, she often let her mind linger on all the many possibilities for the life they would make together after the war, and every single one of them excited her. How could she possibly decide?

He smiled. 'I don't want to take you away from your family, Peg. I've got no one in the States I want to go back to, no one there who really cares if I live or die except for my sister, and I don't even know where she is any more. It would be nice to be part of a family, and for our kids to have a grandad.'

She laughed, delighted by the thought of the children they would have together, a whole life to be lived in each other's company. And though she knew that very soon Zack would take his place in the fast-growing numbers of Americans flying dangerous missions over Europe, she did not allow herself to think about it.

For now, at least, the war was far away and could not touch them.

Chapter Sixteen

1943

Zack got away from the base as much as he could, and they stole every moment to be together, sharing secret kisses in the cellar and the kitchen when her father was busy in the bar, or walking in the cold winter nights, nestled close. Now and then, they risked creeping to her attic room once the pub had closed to hold each other through each rare and precious night they spent together.

If her father noticed, he said nothing, and as the weeks slid by the two men seemed gradually to make their peace, sharing brief snippets of conversation across the bar that slowly lengthened as her father's coldness began at last to thaw. It turned out they shared a common interest in motorcycles, and though Zack hadn't owned a bike since he left his home town for New York, he had kept up a keen knowledge through magazines and talking to other men who shared his passion. It warmed Peggy's heart to see them together, relief etched deep inside her, and she would find herself smiling at the sight of the two of them poring over ancient magazines her father unearthed from somewhere, or discussing the finer points of engines she knew nothing about. Then, one after-noon, when her father led the airman out to the garage to examine the long-neglected BSA that was beginning to rust from disuse, she knew Zack had won him over completely.

Later that night they sat together in the kitchen upstairs drinking tea after the pub had closed. They both knew that this was a golden time, stolen moments of peace before he went to war, and Peggy still refused to think about it, praying for a miracle.

Zack ran his fingertips up and down the sides of his cup. She watched their movement, mesmerised by their elegance, his long narrow fingers pale and beautiful. He had played in the pub that night – soft, moody jazz that had made her feel wistful for some unknown thing, stirring unfamiliar feelings of longing and regret. She had sung along to a couple of songs when she knew the words – Peggy Lee numbers that could almost break her heart.

Now, in the silence of the kitchen, a tension descended. From the bar downstairs they heard the sound of the clock chiming ten and the clunk of her father locking up, the heavy bolts that he had once closed against her shooting home. That seemed long ago now, in another time, though only a few short weeks had passed since then. How quickly a life could change, Peggy thought.

Zack looked up from his contemplation of the tea, and his eyes were shadowed with an expression she was uncertain how to read. Reluctance? Sorrow? It was difficult to say. Her mouth went dry.

'What is it?' she whispered. 'What's wrong?'

He let out a long breath between his lips. 'I'm not supposed to say anything,' he began, and she shook her head.

'Then don't.' She placed her hand on his wrist and felt the muscle moving beneath the skin as his fingers shifted up and down on the cup. His skin was warm to her touch. 'You don't need to.'

She held his gaze for a moment, saw the pain in his eyes, and there was no need for him to say anything else. She knew what he wanted to say: that the bombers were about to start flying in earnest, and he was going to war. Her breath seemed to leave her body, hollowing out her insides. She didn't know how she would manage to live and breathe in the hours that he was gone. How could you learn to live with so much fear and dread? How could the world continue to turn while he was in such danger?

'I won't be able to see you as much,' he said softly, 'and that's the worst part.'

She shook her head again, mute with sorrow, throat constricting with the tears she was trying vainly to quell.

'Don't cry,' he murmured, and lifted his hand to wipe at her cheek with the tip of his thumb.

With his words, she crumbled, all the fear she had held inside all this time forcing its way to the surface. She lowered her face into her hands, still fighting against the sobs, furious with herself for weeping. Zack got up and moved round the table to hold her, and she clung to him as if she would never let him go. He stroked her hair with his beautiful fingers and all she could think of was how much she loved him, and the bone-deep fear of losing him.

Behind her, she heard the kitchen door swing open, and with a sniff and a savage wipe of her face with her hands, she stood back from Zack and faced her father.

'I'm sorry,' he said. 'Am I interrupting something?'

'No, not at all,' she answered quickly. 'I'm just being a cry-baby.'

Zack reached for her fingers and squeezed them, and she looked up at him with a rueful smile.

'No, you're not. Not at all. I'd be beside myself too if you were flying into war.'

Her father nodded his understanding and backed away. 'I'll leave you to it.'

'No. There's tea in the pot. Sit down.'

With a glance to Zack for confirmation, her father slid into his seat at the table, and they began to talk of other things.

Two days later she woke in the grey of the early morning when the roar of the bombers shattered the dawn. She was accustomed to the thunder of the B17s, a constant punctuation to her daily life; conversations halting, the rattle of windows. But she had never heard this relentless, endless din, as though the skies had cracked open and unleashed the end of days. She lay frozen and shaking, barely able to breathe as the whole house vibrated in the wash of so many bombers so close overhead.

Her mind filled with images of Zack in his little Plexiglas dome at the rear of the plane, watching the village disappear as they flew to who knew where, away from her. He'd rarely talked about his life as a gunner – in the glow of their love for each other, neither had wanted to bring the war any closer, aware it would come to them soon enough. But now that it was here at last, she wished she had asked him more. It might help a little to understand more of what he was going through: she could ride along with him in her mind, the two of them together in her thoughts at least.

Slowly, slowly, the thunder began to diminish, like a storm that rolled away across the countryside, but she lay still unmoving in her bed, unable to summon the will to get up and face the day. How could she go about her normal tasks when Zack was in a bomber over Europe, fighting for his life? How could she even begin to function? Her gaze remained trained on the window, her mind's eye following the phalanx of bombers out over the coast, and from along the landing she heard her father open and close the bathroom door. She should get up, she thought, and make tea and breakfast, but her limbs refused to obey her.

When her father's footsteps had finally faded down the stairs, she took hold of her resolve and forced herself out of bed. Her ears were still ringing with the echo of the bombers, and though she shook her head gently to clear it, it made no difference. Then, taking a long slow breath to find the will to keep going, she swung herself out of bed, went to the dresser, and began to get dressed.

The whole village was sombre, the usual lunchtime light-heartedness in the pub overshadowed by the knowledge of the raid. Though most of the villagers barely knew the Americans as individuals, the airmen had become a familiar sight, part of the landscape, and even those locals most resentful of their presence couldn't deny the gravity of this day. They knew from the losses at other bases that not all the bombers that had taken off that morning would make it home. And not all of the men aboard them would live to see another day. So the chatter in the pub was muted, and Peggy went about her work in anxious silence.

She was on her way to visit Sylvia after the pub had closed when the drone of the first returning airplane disturbed the silence. She stopped in the road, and others did the same, coming to their doorways to see them home, their own fates seemingly tied to those of the airmen.

The drone swelled into the customary roar as the ragged formation hove into view, and Peggy shielded her eyes with her hand against the glare of the sky as she lifted her head to watch them. One was trailing a cloud of smoke, another's engine spluttered and coughed. One was missing a chunk from its mid-section. Zack had told her once that B17s could still fly when there was almost nothing left of them – that they were the hardiest of aircraft. Watching them now, she understood – she could barely believe they were still airborne.

Sylvia appeared at her side.

'Come inside,' she mouthed through the din. 'I'll make us some tea.'

Peggy let herself be guided into the post office and upstairs to the kitchen on the first floor where she sat at the table, still listening to the endless rumble of the returning planes. She wanted to run to the base and find him, to know that he was safe. But he had said he would come to her as soon as he could, and so there was nothing else she could do but wait. Sylvia leaned back against the counter, head tilted.

With an effort of will Peggy smiled at her friend. 'How are you?'

'I'm all right,' Sylvia replied, returning the smile. 'You know me. Never down for long.'

Peggy nodded. It was true. Sylvia could make the best of any situation and find joy in the most unlikely of places. Peggy couldn't have counted the number of times they had been in trouble together at school for laughing at inopportune moments, and she wouldn't have traded in a single one of them, in spite of the detentions and the letters home.

At last the drone began to dwindle, and they no longer had to shout to make themselves heard, but half of Peggy's mind was still with them, willing Zack to safety. The kettle boiled and Sylvia made the tea.

'How's Zack?' she asked, looking up, and Peggy heard the effort in the bright, cheery tone. 'How are the wedding plans?'

'He's fine,' she replied. 'We're still waiting for permission. And now that the missions have started, we have no idea when it will be. I suppose we'll just have to wait.'

Her friend looked up from the pot and gave her a wry smile. 'War is hell.'

'So they say.'

They drank their tea and in the wake of the bombers the silence seemed loud.

'Did you know that Jim came to see me?' Sylvia lifted a sardonic eyebrow. 'Begging for my forgiveness.'

'I hope you didn't give it to him.'

'Of course not,' her friend said. 'But I let him think I might for a while. It was very satisfying to see him grovel.'

'What did he say? What possible defence could he give you?' Peggy could hardly believe his audacity.

'He said he would leave his wife for me. That after the war he'd marry me instead.'

'And he expected you to believe him?'

Sylvia laughed. 'He really did.' She took a mouthful of tea.

'But I'm glad he came because I saw him for the cad he actually is, and it felt good to turn him away.' She lowered her eyes away, hoping to hide the shadow of her heartbreak, but Peggy saw it anyway, and reached across to take her hand. With the touch, Sylvia raised her head again with a bright and determined smile.

'Well, there are plenty more fish in the sea, as my mother says.'

'That's the spirit,' Peggy said gently.

A truck started up in the street outside and the roar of its engine cut through the peace. Peggy flicked a glance to the window.

'I should get going. In case Zack comes.' Though she guessed it would take a while she couldn't bear the thought of not being there to meet him, and a sudden panic thrilled through her blood.

Sylvia nodded and said nothing, but simply cradled the teacup between her hands and gazed towards the window, as if she were dreaming of escape.

'You know where I am if you need me,' Peggy said from the door, and Sylvia turned with a half-smile of acknowledgement.

She hurried down the stairs, eager now to get to the pub, to be home and waiting. But the beaten look on Sylvia's face filled her with sorrow. Her friend had always been so vital and lively, always with a smile and a laugh: in all the years they had been friends she had seemed invincible, as though nothing the world could throw at her would ever dent the joy she found in life. But she had fallen hard for Jim and her heart was utterly broken. It was pitiful to see, and she hated the American anew.

Her own fate could just have easily been the same, she reflected. If she hadn't met Zack, she could have fallen for a different man, a man like Jim. Shuddering at the possibility, she whispered a small prayer of thanks to a god she didn't believe in for her own good fortune in finding Zack, and wandered home in the drizzle.

Chapter Seventeen

1943

The pub hadn't long opened its doors and the place was still empty when the whole crew of the *American Maiden* barrelled through the doors. Peggy's heart dropped inside her with relief when she saw him and he went to her straight away and held her tightly, his arms strong around her. Behind them, the others were ordering beer, loud and cheery. But she could hear the weariness that shadowed their voices, celebration tainted with exhaustion.

She stepped back and looked into Zack's face, and though he smiled his lovely smile, there was a new sadness at the edges of his eyes and a pallor to his skin she had not seen before. She lifted a hand and smoothed back the strand of his hair that had fallen forward across his brow. He closed his eyes briefly at her touch.

'How was it?' she asked and wished she had said something else – it seemed such a trite thing to ask.

He shook his head as though he had no words to explain, and then looked up with nod of thanks as Freddie handed him a beer. The pilot, who was their leader, raised his bottle.

'To the *American Maiden*,' he toasted. 'And all who fly in her.'

The men lifted their bottles in salute, briefly silent. Peggy cast her eyes across the men. She hadn't met the whole crew before, only the gunners who sometimes came and drank with Zack and Freddie, and they nodded to her now in greeting. She forced herself to smile as Zack took her hand to lead her towards the others to introduce her, and she was conscious of her own weariness, the fear she had held at bay all through the hours of the raid draining away to leave a residue of dread she suspected would never leave. One mission down, she thought. But how many more to go?

She greeted the others in a daze, and perhaps on another occasion they would have talked more easily, but the night was not about her: these men had faced their first trial and survived, and to all of them but Zack she was an afterthought to their need for celebration.

'Should I go?' she asked him softly. 'So you can be with your friends. I feel like I'm in the way.'

Zack turned to her with a small smile that crinkled his eyes. The back of his hand brushed against hers.

'Thank you. Just for a little while. And then I'll be all yours again.'

She kissed him on the cheek, which drew a cheer and a low whistle from a couple of the others, and left him to join her father behind the bar. They stood side by side, watching the airmen as they laughed and joked and rehashed the mission over and over again, a bond between them now that only war could have forged. Then her father turned abruptly away, and began to wipe the counter down, though it was already clean.

'Are you all right, Dad?' she asked.

He paused in his work but did not look at her.

'I remember that feeling.' He jerked his head towards the airmen. 'The relief to have survived another day. It's heady and exhilarating, a surge of emotion like I've never felt before or since. While it lasts, you feel like a god.'

She was silent. He had never once talked to her before about his own experience in the Great War, though she knew he bore a scar the length of one thigh that he steadfastly refused to admit gave him pain now and then. She had long since given up commenting when she saw him limping or grimacing in pain.

'I wonder how many of the others didn't make it,' he murmured, more to himself than to her so that she wasn't even sure she heard him right. Then, letting the cloth he was holding fall on to the counter, he turned away and disappeared through the doorway that led out behind the bar.

Slowly, the men's bright excitement settled into quieter conversation, but she sensed they were still going over the events of the day and so she kept her distance. A few times Zack turned his head from the chatter and gave her a smile while she went about her work, waiting patiently. Other customers came in and gave the crew appreciative nods. Now that the raids had begun the airmen's presence had taken on a new and graver significance. They were no longer young men in training, awaiting their chance to prove themselves. They were fighting for Europe's freedom and the villagers were proud to be associated with them in however small a way: they belonged to the village – their boys.

The night remained quiet, and her father came and went through the evening but said no more about the war. He had a still and determined look about him that discouraged questions, and she guessed the airmen's celebrations had woken dormant memories he rarely visited. She wished he would talk to her about them – a problem shared is a problem halved, her mother used to say. But she knew beyond all doubt that he would never say a word about them to her or to anyone. He would take those griefs and hurts to his grave, unspoken. For the first time in her memory he retired early with a mumbled good night, and left her to close up.

Finally, the airmen got up to go. Zack spoke briefly in an undertone to the pilot, who looked towards her with a smile before turning once more to Zack with a nod.

'Back by dawn though, okay?'

'Yes, sir.'

The Americans were the last customers to leave, and Zack did not go with them. Out of habit she scanned the pub for her father, unsure how he would react if he knew. But he was upstairs, out of sight, and so she locked the door as Zack picked up the empty bottles and took them through to the back to be washed and returned to the brewery the following morning. Then they stood in the middle of the empty pub and, for the first time, she felt awkward in his presence, not knowing what to say. She had so many questions but no words to frame them, and so she said nothing at all.

After a moment, he reached out for her hand and she took it, but neither of them made another move to go. Then, with a quick glance to make sure they were still alone, he drew her towards him so that their bodies were just touching, and their faces close enough to kiss with just a little tilt of their heads.

Still they hesitated, as if the knowledge of the raid sat between them as a tangible presence that had changed the way they were with each other. In the corner the clock struck the half hour, and finally, she conjured words to her lips.

'Shall we go upstairs?'

He nodded, and so she led him out behind the bar and crept up the stairs to her bedroom beneath the roof.

They made love with quiet, urgent passion, and she could not hold him close enough, nor draw him deep enough inside her to satisfy her need for him.

One mission done.

The knowledge played in her head over and over. How many more to go? Even in their passion, the fear refused to be silenced.

Afterwards, she lay with her head on his shoulder, and her fingers gently smoothed the soft hair on his chest and the narrow line of it that led down across his belly. She was aware of the solidity of his muscles against her – firm and full of life – and she nestled her body in closer and wrapped her leg around his so that he turned to her.

'Are you okay?'

She lifted her head to look at him, taking in those soft green eyes with the lines that appeared at the corners when he smiled that she loved so much, and the stubble on his chin that was rough against her hair.

'I'm afraid,' she said. Because in the end, everything else hinged on that one pivotal emotion. No matter how she tried to dress it up, the terror of losing him was lodged deep in her core, inescapable.

'Me too,' he replied.

'What was it like?'

'It's hard to explain. It's very strange up there. It's kind of like being in a dream and at the same time, it's the most real thing I've ever done.'

She nodded, though she was no nearer to understanding. Only the men who flew could ever really understand, she knew, and the strength of the bonds that connected them were unfathomable to those on the outside.

'Did ...' She stopped, hesitant to ask. Then, because the need to know was almost consuming, she went on. 'Did everyone come back?'

She felt his chest heave beneath her as he drew in a breath before he answered.

'Not everyone.'

'I'm so sorry.'

'It's war, and I'm just glad it wasn't me.' His fingertips brushed against the skin of her arm, tickling. 'Is that a terrible thing to say?'

'If it is I'm just as guilty,' she replied. 'I think it's human nature, though, isn't it?'

Surely it was. To be glad to be the one who had survived when others had died, to be relieved when the person you loved the most was the one who came home.

'I guess,' he said.

She said nothing more, but only reached across to turn out the lamp before nestling in close to him again. Then, in the quiet dark, they fell quickly into sleep.

. . .

In her dream she is swimming in the river she used to swim in as a child, playing in the shallows, the water biting cold against her skin and delicious in its chill.

A warm summer sun lights a clear blue sky, and the banks are soft with green grass and daisies. It is a perfect day. There is a picnic rug and a basket and she remembers that she came there with Zack to celebrate something. Though she knows it is important, she can't recall now what it was. How can she have forgotten?

Desperate to know, she looks around for Zack to ask him, expecting to see him in the water alongside her or lying on the rug on the bank. Wheeling slowly in the water, she searches along the riverbank with a growing sense of dread.

When her eyes find him at last, he is on the far side of the river, a long way away, and his outline is blurred as though she were looking into the sun, his face in shadow. She tries to call out to him but her voice makes no sound so she raises her arm to beckon him, but he still seems not to notice her.

Frantic now for his attention, she stands up in the water and starts to wade towards him, but although the river is only shallow she makes no progress at all, and no matter how hard she tries to reach him she is still no nearer to the opposite shore – the gulf between them is impossible to cross.

Chapter Eighteen

1995

Georgia gave the pot of soup a final stir, turned off the gas and cast an approving glance across the kitchen, where the plates and dishes were laid out in preparation, the counters clean and bright. Her kitchen, she thought, and she liked it. It was a shame Grandpa couldn't see her there – he would have liked to know she had moved back to the village. He would have come in sometimes and had a half-pint and a pasty for his lunch. The thought of it made her smile.

Wandering out to the bar with a tea towel still in her hand she saw that it was all but empty, a quiet Monday lunchtime. Two of the regulars were nursing half-pints at their usual table in the corner, and Ben was perched on a stool at the bar on the customers' side with the order book in front of him. He was tapping the end of his pen on the page, and gazing at something beyond the far wall that only he could see. She watched him for a moment, observing once again the clear green eyes and the sharp outline of his jaw. It was a good face, she thought, both handsome and kind.

Catching her movement at the edge of his attention, he turned abruptly.

'All done?' he asked.

She nodded. 'If the hordes descend, there will be food.'

He slanted a wry glance to the two old fellows in the corner with their half pints and laughed.

'Why don't you sit down? Prepare yourself for the onslaught.'

He gestured to the stool beside him and she slid onto it, returning his laugh with a smile. They sat for a moment in silence, both searching for something to say beyond the demands of the pub. So far they had rarely ever talked of anything but work or idle chit-chat, and she was beginning to wonder if he was keeping her at arm's length for a reason: she had hoped to get to know him better by now. But even so, there was something about his reserve she found attractive; it carried a quiet confidence that he had no need to explain himself, and it was completely different to Scott's bluff patter to anyone who would listen. His self-sufficiency was intriguing, arousing her curiosity, and she was eager to spend more time in his company.

'How's your grandmother doing?' Ben asked, after a moment. 'It must be hard being widowed after so many years of marriage.'

'Surprisingly well,' Georgia replied. 'But she's always been an independent spirit. She's been telling me about when she was younger.'

'Oh?' He tilted his head with interest, waiting for her to go on.

'Did you know she lived here, in the pub? Her father was

the landlord during the war and I'm doing more or less the same job that she did.'

'No, I didn't know that.' He grinned. 'That's incredible! It's a small world.'

'The pasties are her recipe from then.'

He nodded his head in acknowledgement, a smile still at the corners of his mouth as his eyes met hers, and she thought again how much she liked him. Turning a beermat between her fingers on the bar, Georgia lowered her gaze away to the carpet at her feet so he wouldn't be able to read the thoughts behind it, reluctant to give her feelings away just yet.

'And how are you?' he asked then. 'Are you settling in okay? No regrets about leaving London?'

She looked up quickly and met the question in his eyes with a ready smile, pleased by his interest.

'I'm fine,' she said. 'No regrets at all. That life already feels like ancient history and I'm happy to say I don't miss it a single bit.'

It was true – she had barely even thought of London or Scott these last few weeks, and the person she had been before seemed like a stranger she wasn't sure she even recognised. For the first time in years she realised she was happy.

'I'm glad,' he replied, and in the pause that followed she thought that might be the end of the conversation. She searched her mind for something to say to keep them talking, but it was Ben who broke the silence.

He said, 'You grew up here, didn't you?'

She nodded, unsure how much to tell him: at times those years were still painful to recall, memories she rarely allowed herself to visit.

'I moved here when I was twelve,' she said. 'My mum was

killed in a car crash and I didn't have a dad, so I came to live here with my grandparents.'

'That must have been hard.'

'It was, especially at first.' She stopped, trying to sort her feelings into the right words. 'But when I was little, Mum and I moved around a lot – she could never seem to stay anywhere for more than a few months, so Sutton Heath was actually the first place that ever felt like home. I never understood what drove her – I was just a child, with a child's understanding …' She shrugged, and let out a long low breath to steady herself. It was a long time since she had allowed herself to think of those years, and the memories still had the power to kindle the same sense of helpless sadness she had known as a girl.

'Was she just restless?' Ben asked, his voice gentle, and she could hear the same incomprehension in his question that had always haunted her.

She shook her head. 'I don't think so. I think it was more than that. It was like she was running away from something, or someone. Nana told me only very recently that Mum had been involved with some bad types for a while – so perhaps she really was trying to outrun her past. I guess I'll never know.'

'I'm sorry,' Ben said. 'I shouldn't have asked. I didn't mean to upset you.'

'That's okay,' she answered quickly. 'It's a long time ago now, and I'm just thankful for the home my grandparents gave me. I was very happy with them once I settled down, very lucky to have them.'

Georgia put on a bright smile, and in the silence she wondered if she should have said so much – she didn't want to frighten him away with tales of woe from her childhood. She was aware of his gaze as it rested on her face and after a moment she lifted her eyes to meet his, fearing to see judgement or pity. But she saw only kindness and a faint light of curiosity, as if he would like to know more about her, and she was warmed by the glow of his attention. There was a comfortable silence, and she was glad she had told him.

'What did you do before the pub?' she asked him then, shifting the focus away from herself.

'I was a chef,' he replied. 'I worked in hotels and restaurants here and there – London mostly, travelled overseas a bit. It was fun for a while, but it wasn't really what I wanted to do – long hours, high stress.'

She tried to imagine him in a hectic hotel kitchen and failed – that person seemed a world away from the soft spoken landlord of the pub she was coming to know.

'So how did you end up here?'

'I grew up in Cambridge, and I heard about this place by chance one time when I was visiting home. I drove out and had a look at it, and it just seemed too good to refuse. And ...' He paused. 'It was a good time for a new start.'

She gave him a quizzical look and waited, hoping for more, but he only laughed.

'But that's a story for another time,' he said.

A new silence fell, and she was content as they looked over the expanse of the pub with appreciation – it seemed it was a sanctuary for them both.

The sudden jangle of the bell as the door juddered open made them jump in surprise, and they looked at each other and laughed. Then, turning to the door, they watched as a group of walkers in hiking boots bustled in with backpacks and walking sticks, faces flushed.

'Do you do food?' one of them asked.

'We do,' Ben answered. 'Take a seat.'

Then, with another shared smile that made Georgia feel warm inside, they got down from their stools and went back to work.

The door was on the latch as usual when she got home from work that afternoon, and Georgia hung her coat on the hook behind it. Despite the quiet start to the day it had turned out to be a busy lunchtime after all, and she was eager for the warmth of the kitchen and a cup of tea. Her grandmother was sitting at the table with the crossword, but when she looked up to welcome her granddaughter home, her eyes seemed to have lost a little of their usual sparkle, dark shadows underneath them.

'Are you all right, Nana?' Georgia asked, frowning with worry. 'You look tired.'

'I'm fine,' her grandmother answered, with a shake of her head. 'I just didn't sleep well. I had bad dreams. Dreams I haven't had for years.'

'What kind of dreams?'

'About the war,' Nana said, in a tone that seemed to close the conversation. Then she got up from her place at the table to set the kettle on the stove in spite of Georgia's protestations she could do it herself.

Realising it was a battle she would not win, Georgia sat down as she was told and watched her grandmother moving around the kitchen. In spite of her years, she was still an attractive woman, grey hair drawn back neatly into a ponytail and her skin barely wrinkled beyond the laugh lines and the three faint creases that crossed her forehead. Not for the first time, Georgia tried to imagine her as a young woman during the war, working in the kitchen at the pub where Georgia worked now, making the same sandwiches, pasties and soup the Queen's Head had served since time immemorial. But despite all that her grandmother had told her, it was still hard to picture it – a different world, a world at war.

'A letter came,' Nana said, looking over her shoulder from her place at the sink. 'On the table there.'

'Who from?' Georgia sat up straighter, her tiredness forgotten in an instant as she noticed for the first time the envelope that was propped against the salt and pepper jars.

'A Louise Bennett, in America,' Nana said. 'It's addressed to you, so I thought I'd better wait.'

It was fat with paper, and her heart jumped in her chest as she reached for it. Zack's sister's name had been Louise, and though Georgia had written a letter to the Eldon family care of the post office in Bliss, she hadn't dared to hope that it would actually find its way home. Was this a reply from her? Excitement prickled across her skin.

'Oh, Nana, how did you stop yourself from opening it?' She laughed and picked up a knife to slice the envelope open. It parted with a satisfying rip. 'You didn't have to wait.'

'I wanted to,' Nana said. 'I thought we should read it together.'

Georgia slid the folded sheets of paper out of the envelope and straightened them out with her fingers. Then she picked up the top sheet, and as Nana stood behind her to read over her shoulder, she began to read it aloud.

Dear Georgia and Peggy,

Thank you for your letter, which I'm astonished to say found its way all the way to me here in San Diego. What a surprise! I really don't know where to begin to reply to all your questions, so please bear with me as I try to answer what I can.

I was delighted to hear from you and your grandmother. I've sometimes wondered over the years whatever happened to the girl at the pub that Zack had written to tell me he was sweet on. I still have the letter he wrote to me and I've enclosed a photocopy. It was the only one I ever got from him after he shipped out to Europe – for a long while after I left Bliss I moved from place to place, until I finally settled here in California after the war and married my husband, Duncan. So perhaps he wrote again but they never found me.

I didn't go back home for years – I'm sure Zack told you about the kind of childhood we had – and there was nothing to go back to. But last year Dad died and so I went to the house for the first time in decades to sort out his things. Who would have thought a man who drank that hard could have lived so long? Duncan always said his organs must have been pickled and preserved.

I have to admit it was very painful to return. I loved my brother dearly, and it was the last place we were together. I never blamed him for leaving – he bore the brunt of Dad's temper far more often than I did, and when he went he said he would get me out too as soon as he could.

Then the war came along and upset just about everyone's plans.

The house was exactly as I'd remembered it – an unkempt shack with a rusting roof, junk strewn about the yard, the gate still off its hinges. I spent days digging through all his belongings. Dad was a hoarder, and there was a lot to sort out. I suppose I hoped I'd find something worth saving in amongst it all. But there was really nothing – just a few old photographs of us as kids, (I'll get some copies made and send them to you), the rusted remains of Zack's motorbike, Mum's wedding ring.

I'd almost given up looking when I finally came across the only thing in all that rubbish that was truly worth saving – a shoebox in the garage stuffed with telegrams, letters and papers, and underneath it all, Zack's dog tags, a St Christopher, and his medal.

I suppose Dad was still listed as next of kin. Of course, he never told me about any of it. The only thing he ever wrote to me about was the telegram that told us Zack was dead.

Georgia stopped reading and looked up at her grandmother, still standing behind her with one hand gripping Georgia's shoulder.

'Do you want to sit down?'

Nana nodded slightly and slid into the chair beside Georgia's. Both of them were barely breathing and, with one more glance at each other, they began to read again.

I've enclosed copies of the letters his crew mates wrote, and their testimony of the bravery that earned him his Congressional Medal of Honor. If you loved my brother as I did then I'm sure you don't need a medal to know that he was a hero – in his quiet way, he was the toughest, kindest, bravest man I ever met. But the documents enclosed will give you some understanding of Zack's final hours, and the lives he saved by his actions.

In the new year, my husband has plans to travel to Europe for business. I thought that if you'd like, I could accompany him and we could spend some time together? I would so very much like to meet the girl my brother loved, and his granddaughter. And of course I would love to see his medal in its rightful place with you.

Now that you have my address, I look forward very much to hearing from you again soon. How very wonderful that you contacted me after all these years. I can't wait to meet you.

Much love,
Louise x

Georgia lowered the letter to the table and tried and failed to blink back her tears. But even through the haze of them she could see her grandmother's still pale face as she grappled with the meaning of the words in front of her.

'He was a hero,' Georgia whispered, wiping at her tears.

'I know,' Nana said. 'But it still doesn't bring him back. It doesn't make up for all the years we never had together.'

She began to cry in earnest then, sobs wracking her delicate frame, and Georgia wrapped her arms around her and held her close.

'I'm sorry,' she said. 'I shouldn't have tried to find out.'

She felt awful, guilt for her grandmother's distress a physical ache.

Nana sat back abruptly and dragged at the tears on her cheeks with impatient fingers, sniffing and blinking to clear her eyes.

'Don't be ridiculous,' she said. She reached for a tissue from the box and dabbed at her eyes. 'It hurts. Of course it hurts. But you've connected me to Zack's sister, and in that pile of paper there …' She gestured to the little stack of photocopies on the table. '… are the details of how the man I loved actually died. It means the world to me to know, and to know that others recognised him as a hero too.'

Georgia nodded, relieved, and the two women sat in

silence for a while in the quiet afternoon. From far off in the distance, they could hear the low drone of a jet plane heading towards Luton or Stansted. Georgia wondered if it reminded Nana of the B17s, engines roaring close overhead.

She got up to make more tea, and her eyes glanced across all the photocopies on the table that Louise had sent. She could barely contain her excitement to read them and put together the last pieces of the puzzle, and she struggled to quell her impatience. Like a child before Christmas, she had to fight against an urge to just stretch across and lift the first sheet from the pile. But there would be time enough, and her grandmother was still reeling from Louise's letter.

Nana must have sensed her eagerness.

'I know you must be very curious,' she said, 'but I'd like to read them by myself first of all. I'm sorry, I hope you understand.'

She looked up at her granddaughter, who was rinsing out the tea cups at the sink, and her eyes were sad and tired. She looked old suddenly, Georgia thought, as though all the sorrow of the past had caught up with her at last.

'Of course I understand,' Georgia said, with a small smile that she hoped would mask her disappointment. 'Of course.'

She watched as her grandmother got up from her chair and picked up the sheaf of papers, clutching them to her chest like something infinitely precious. Then, returning her granddaughter's smile with a weary one of her own, she took the letters upstairs to her bedroom to piece together the final hours of Zack's life.

Chapter Nineteen

1943

He should not have been flying. He should have still been sleeping and warm in his bed in the hut he shared with Freddie and the other gunners.

His own airplane, the *American Maiden,* was in for repairs. They had lost an engine on the last run and though no one talked about it, the crew was relieved to be out of the fight even for a short while – a brief reprieve in the endless round of missions that seemed to get longer, harder, and ever more dangerous.

It was just a question of odds, Freddie said. The more times you go, the higher the chances you won't make it back. Zack knew his friend was right but he tried not to think about it. The odds were the same each and every time, he told himself. And so far, they had been lucky.

But last night the tail gunner of the *Fine and Dandy* had broken his arm when his bicycle skidded and sent him sprawling on the frozen mud and Zack, caught in the wrong place at the wrong time on his way back from spending the evening with Peggy, had been volunteered to take his place. He had bitten his lip and said nothing, accepting the task without question – someone had to go, after all, so why not him? But all the men hated going out with a different crew, on a different ship. It was a kind of superstition, he supposed, a faith in the circle of luck the men had wound around themselves through all the missions they had flown together. Would the charm still hold without them? He shook his head, berating himself for thinking it – he was in no more danger in the *Fine and Dandy* than he was in the *American Maiden*, but however hard he tried he couldn't make himself believe it.

He knew the guys well enough. Robert Gough, the big and burly pilot with a Boston drawl, and Frank Carter, the bombardier, a wiry guy from Chicago with a dry sense of humour and a reputation for picking fights. The two crews had joined forces for a ball game not so long ago and they won the match, so that had to count for something, surely? He gave his reflection a wry smile in the mirror. Who was he trying to kid? The chances were the same, either way, but he would still feel safer with Tom and Randall in the cockpit, Freddie in the turret, and Harry Woods to navigate them safely home.

Studying the face in the mirror that gazed back at him, he barely recognised it as his own. Clouded eyes with dark circles underneath, and a pallor to his skin he hadn't noticed before – it was the face of an older man. He ran his hand across the stubble on his cheeks and thought of Peggy, who loved him. She would be sleeping now in the soft bed in the attic at the pub he was starting to think of as home. He could imagine living a whole life with her there, taking over the pub in time, and though they had talked of moving to New York or London after the war, he had begun to ache for the peace of a country village life, a quiet life with the woman he loved. He could play piano every night in the pub, he thought, and it would be a good and peaceful existence. The thought of it raised a tired and hopeful smile and, with a sigh, he towelled off his face and headed out into the dark of the early hours to the mess tent for breakfast.

Later, when the guns had been loaded into position on the bomber and the crew was ready, he shared a cigarette with Lyle, the *Fine and Dandy*'s bombardier. It was the only time he ever smoked, this last moment of fresh air with his feet on solid ground – it helped to quell the churning in his guts and the chill that always seemed to shiver through his limbs, whatever the weather. Until today, it had always been Freddie at his side to share it and he cast a wistful glance towards the accommodation huts, where Freddie and the others would be just beginning to stir as the bombers made ready at their hardstands. There wasn't a man on the base who didn't rise from his bed to see the bombers off each morning, the desire for sleep giving way to a visceral need to wish each mission safely home.

Above them, the sky was finally beginning to lighten with the coming dawn, velvet black slowly fading into a dull and dreary grey, the stars going out one by one. The two men smoked in silence, passing the cigarette back and forth between them. There was nothing to say, and the tension stretched tight across the airfield. Despite the clamour of activity – the roar of trucks and the thud of equipment, men shouting last-minute questions and instructions – there always seemed to Zack to be a kind of hush at this moment. No chit-chat. No banter, as every man searched inside himself for the resolve to face what lay ahead.

Then the first engine split the silence and broke the spell. Stamping the butt of the cigarette into the concrete at his feet with his boot, Zack gave Lyle a nod which the other man returned with a tilt of his head before the two of them hauled themselves up through the hatch and into the plane. The smell of it was strangely comforting – the same familiar stench of oil and gas, sweat and fear as the *American Maiden* that made him feel at home. He took a deep breath, and headed along the fuselage towards his place in the rear of the plane to do his pre-flight checks, head ducked and moving stiffly in the heavy heated suit he would plug in once they were airborne and the temperature began to fall.

His station was cramped – little more than a bicycle seat and padded supports to kneel on, armoured plates below the ballistic glass that was his window on to the world, but it still felt to him like the safest place on the ship. Going through the same routine he had done a thousand times before he almost forgot that he was on a different plane – the oxygen regulator, the intercom, the gunsight, were all but identical. It was only when an unfamiliar voice sounded in his headphones that he remembered with a lurch in his guts that he was on the *Fine and Dandy* and not his beloved *American Maiden*.

When he was happy with his checks, he shuffled back out of his section to the ship's waist and exchanged nods of greeting with the other men as they hunkered down to wait for take off. One by one the Fortresses took their turn in the line, thundering down the runway and lurching airborne with reluctance, as though the planes themselves knew what awaited them and had to be coaxed into the air, like race-horses to the starting gates. Heading into the clouds, Zack peered out to take a last look at the village as it rapidly diminished behind him. The red-tiled roof of the pub was easy to pick out, and he let his gaze linger on it as the bomber gained speed and height and the village diminished beneath them. Below that roof in her attic room, Peggy would have woken at the formation's roar, and he let his mind trail across the image – her fair hair messy as she stretched and yawned, the shiver of her body as the cold morning air touched her skin. It was the image he wanted to wake to every day for the rest of his life. With a stab of regret that he wasn't there with her now, he closed his eyes for a moment and sent her a secret, silent kiss. Then, as the clouds gathered around them and the fields of England were lost to his sight, he forced his thoughts away from the woman he loved above all else, and turned them instead towards the mission ahead.

Somewhere out over the English Channel he crawled back into his station and took up his place in the tail, folding his tall frame into the cramped space that had become so familiar through all the months of flying. Running his gloved hands across the cold metal of the guns, he was reassured by the familiar heft of them, and on the go-ahead from the pilot he chambered a round and test-fired them, the gunfire cracking loud above the drone of the engines. Everything was working as it should, but he still couldn't rid himself of that superstitious dread of flying with a different crew.

He wasn't supposed to fly today. He wasn't supposed to be here. And no matter how hard he fought to force the notion out of his mind, it kept up a constant patter in his head.

His thoughts shifted of their own accord to Peggy. She would be in the pub kitchen now, he guessed, already making a start on the soup and the pasties for the day's lunch. He observed her in his mind's eye for a moment, running his gaze across the pale, smooth skin of her cheeks, and the fair hair that always broke loose from its pins. The blue eyes bright with a smile for him, her lips parted ready to kiss.

When they reached enemy skies the intercom fell silent and he lost all track of time. His wristwatch was buried beneath the layers of his heated suit and too hard to get to, but he guessed it didn't matter much anyway. He tried to call images of Peggy to his thoughts again, but she felt like an impossible dream to him now: the world of the *Fine and Dandy* was all that existed.

With a sigh, Zack hauled his attention back to the job in hand, running his gaze across the sky behind the bomber, scanning for incoming fighters. Visibility was poor – the trailing contrails from the formation filled the air and obscured his lines of sight. But he narrowed his eyes and kept searching regardless for the German planes that liked to hide among the trails and give the gunners no warning when they arced into view, guns blazing.

The formation of bombers tightened almost imperceptibly, each plane's guns covering the others. Glancing across to the *Saucy Minx* on their port wing, he could see the gunners in their turrets, searching the sky as he was. It was good to know she was there, her weapons armed and ready.

He only knew they were close to their destination when the ship began to tremble from the flak, the formation losing altitude in preparation for the bomb run. Their target today was a munitions factory near the Baltic coast, and he found himself wondering if the dark puffs of smoke that were beginning to darken the sky around them were from weapons made in the factory they'd been sent to destroy. It gave him a grim sense of satisfaction to think so.

The bomber started to bounce and pitch, and he could hear the patter and tap of shrapnel against the metal of its skin. Then there was a sudden lurch as a piece of flak landed somewhere further forward, and he had to brace himself to remain in position, his left arm slamming into the panels beside him as he almost fell from his stool. A shout came over the intercom. He didn't recognise the voice but he heard the note of panic.

'We've been hit! Trent is down!'

The pilot's voice, calm and soft, responded. 'Lloyd, see what's wrong.'

He listened, heart racing as his eyes searched the sky, watching the shells explode all around them, black clouds of smoke filling his field of vision. The ground was completely obscured and if there were any fighters prowling, he knew he wouldn't see them until it was far too late. But he kept scanning nonetheless, peering through the gaps, the smoke swirling and seeming to breathe in the wash of the formation.

Beside them, the *Saucy Minx* bucked and tilted, dropping height abruptly, and he could not tear his eyes away. She began to tip sideways as though she were trying to balance on the very end of one wing, and he saw the rush of flame that erupted from the starboard side, one engine failing to turn. He could imagine the pilot wrestling to regain control and keep up with the pack, and the lurch of fear that travelled through the crew. The distance between them widened as the badly damaged *Minx* struggled to keep up. Zack willed her to stay close.

'Come on!' he urged beneath his breath. She would be easy pickings for a fighter if she fell too far behind. 'Keep up. Stay with us.'

He had played cards with the *Minx*'s bombardier only two nights before, and the dollars he had won were still on the nightstand beside his bed in the hut back at the base. They had planned to have a rematch, he remembered, before he tried to drag his thoughts away from the memory – it did no good to think like that.

The recollection was cut abruptly short. A sudden shudder shook the plane and somewhere nearby an explosion flared – he never saw what it was but a moment later his whole world seemed to erupt – windows shattered into a thousand pieces, metal twisting. The blast was blinding, deafening, shockwaves cascading through every part of him with a mighty crash that felt like the end of the world, dragging the breath from his body. His lungs burned with heat and a desperate need for air, and his head was filled with shards of bright light, like fireworks in his mind, terrifyingly close.

Then the world seemed to fall silent around him. For what seemed an age, there was no sound, no movement, all breath suspended until he finally heaved in a great chestful of air. With the breath, the racket of the war rushed back at him in a deafening roar that he barely had time to register before another sudden force sent him flying sideways into the side of the plane.

He blinked, trying to clear away the blurriness from his vision, and shook his head against the clamour inside it that rendered it impossible to think. His body was pulsating, his mind foggy and clouded, and he struggled to keep himself upright, muscles like water in his limbs. Mustering all that remained of his strength, he dragged himself back into position, tightened his grip on the gun and hauled the fractured fragments of his thoughts once more towards the sky around him.

The air was bitter cold against his cheeks now that the glass was gone, and the tail of the plane was open to the sky. He was glad for the warmth of the helmet and the goggles he had always hated, but the heated suit was no longer warm, the electrics destroyed by the blast. He scanned the scene behind them, but he could catch no sight of the *Saucy Minx*, no trace of her at all. He hoped she was trailing the formation, too far back to see, but there was no time to wonder as his own ship lurched and bounced again in the flak. Another shell burst somewhere too close and the shockwave juddered, pain slicing through his body as the guns were wrenched from his grip, the world tilting and turning black.

He didn't know how long he was out, but he came round to the sound of a voice in his ear. In his confusion, he thought at first it was Peggy, waking him gently from a deep sleep, and he almost smiled before he realised it was the intercom.

'Pilot to tail – are you okay back there?' Though the voice was in his ear, it seemed to come from very far away.

'I'm okay,' Zack heard himself say, struggling to focus, to pull himself upright.

Was he okay? He wasn't sure. He did a quick mental assessment of his limbs – fingers, toes, arms, legs – they all seemed to be present and correct. His torso throbbed, ribs and flanks as bruised and sore as though he had taken a beating, but he couldn't see any blood. Slowly, the world around him began to clear again, shifting once more into focus, and he cast a look around him. The tail guns were hanging loose now, dislodged from their mount and useless, and there was a massive hole in the skin of the plane beside his seat, so that the tail seemed to be barely connected to the rest of the plane at all. He could see the sky rushing past, littered with swarms of black smoke. He needed to get out of there, he realised, before it broke away entirely and took him with it.

Carefully, he backed out of what was left of the tail, but he was awkward and bulky in his heated suit and parachute harness, which caught on the twisted metal and halted his progress. For what seemed like an age he fought with the tangled strap until he finally managed to wrench it free with a rip and continued on his crawl towards the waist. Trailing his bottle of oxygen, the bucking of the plane made it slow going. Twice he banged his head so that it spun again and his vision blurred, and but eventually he made it. The two gunners were on the floor, one of them bent over the other.

'Is he okay?'

The gunner looked up in surprise and shook his head. Zack recognised him as the man who had played in goal in their match together – Lloyd, Zack remembered, from Philadelphia.

He crouched down to help. Trent's eyes were flickering and he was barely conscious. Blood oozed through the fabric of his pants, and Lloyd was pressing on the wound.

'I'll get the first-aid kit,' Zack mouthed, and hurried forward.

He had returned in a moment, and it was only when he took off his gloves to unbuckle Trent's parachute harness that he saw his own blood. Surprised, he peeled back his sleeve to find a gash on his forearm that was bleeding heavily. He almost laughed – how could a man have a wound that bad and not even know?

Then he turned again to care for Trent, teasing the gunner's harness gently away, cutting the fabric and applying a field dressing to stem the worst of the bleeding, before he did what he could to cover his own wound. Now that he knew it was there, it had started to throb, and shards of pain seared through him with every movement of his arm.

The plane gave a sudden lurch upwards and the two men staggered, but as he felt the ship begin to tilt he understood that they had dropped their bombs and were turning to go home. Perhaps, he thought, they might make it back after all. Perhaps tonight he would play piano in the pub with Peggy. They would play "As Time Goes By", he thought, and briefly he was there, the title refrain sweet on Peggy's lips. But the hope was short lived as a burst of gunfire raked the side of the ship and Lloyd fell to the floor like a stone. Zack glanced out past the silent waist guns and caught a glimpse of an ME109 as it hurtled past them.

'Shit!'

He knelt to Lloyd, who was pale and shaking, but still alive. Just. 'Are you okay?'

The other man said nothing, and hurriedly Zack stripped away the gunner's harness and jacket, trying to get to the wound. He found a deep slash across Lloyd's torso, and once more reached for the first-aid kit.

'I'm going to give you some morphine,' he shouted, and Lloyd nodded vaguely as Zack stabbed the little needle into his chest.

He was getting good at this, he thought, as unwrapped the last of the dressings in the first aid kit: he should have been a medic. It seemed to take forever, and though he guessed there would be other, smaller wounds besides, the German fighter plane was circling again and he needed to get to the guns very soon or they would all be in trouble. He covered Lloyd with his jacket against the cold then hurled himself towards the other man's gun.

He reached it too late. The fighter had already strafed one wing and as the German banked and turned to come in again, the bomber's fuel tanks erupted into a burst of flames that ripped along the wing and into the fuselage in seconds. Zack shielded his eyes as the force flung him backwards. He landed hard against the floor and pain screamed through his arm. He fought for purchase, struggling to regain his feet, but beneath him the ship gave another violent shudder, veering sharply as the pilot battled to retain control. Scrambling on all fours to get to the two wounded men, he managed to drag them clear of the flames then set about trying to put out the fire.

Barely a moment later the order came over the intercom to bail out. Zack looked at the two wounded men, whose parachutes he had removed to get to their wounds. Trent was watching him with feverish and frightened eyes, and Zack untangled the harness from where he had thrown it in his haste before, hands clumsy and shaking as he separated out the straps and gently helped the other man into it. Fastening the buckles with fingers that were slippery with sweat and blood, he placed Trent's arm over his shoulder and raised him to a sitting position. He didn't know what was happening in other parts of the ship – the fire had taken hold, and he hoped the others further forward had managed to get out.

The ball-turret gunner had scrambled out from his position beneath the plane and was making straight for the hatch. He was already at its edge before he seemed to notice Zack and the others. For what seemed like a long time the two men locked eyes, and Zack couldn't read the other man's expression. Was he going to help, or just save himself? The gunner looked once more towards the hatch before, with a sigh, he turned back. Then, between them, the two men managed to haul Trent to his feet and manoeuvre him to the opening. Zack watched as they both bailed out in quick succession one after the other.

When they had gone, he staggered back and away like a drunkard as the plane bucked and shifted underfoot. The fuselage seemed to be melting all around him, threatening to tear the plane in half. Carefully skirting the pockets of flame, Zack began to search for Lloyd's harness among the heap of discarded flying clothes and blankets. He couldn't find it. He dragged at the pile, hands frantically scrabbling to unravel it, supposing it had become tangled up with them, but it wasn't there. It had to be. It had to. It couldn't have disappeared. He grimaced at the heat as he cast a desperate glance around the fuselage and wiped the sweat from his eyes, before at last, he glimpsed the edge of it. Briefly he was elated, but as he reached towards it with the beginnings of a smile he saw that it was already blackened by fire and half destroyed.

'Shit!'

He let out a long low breath and looked at Lloyd, who was just a kid really, barely even old enough to shave. The boy was shivering, clammy and pale with shock. He couldn't just leave him here to die. For the length of an outward breath he hesitated, digging inside to find his courage. Even an undamaged parachute could only hold one man, and though the part of him that wanted desperately to live, to spend a whole life with Peggy, briefly toyed with the idea of jumping out together, he knew it would simply kill them both. It was him or Lloyd. He was aware of the other man watching him, terrified. But when Zack began to step out of his own harness the gunner began to shake his head.

'You don't have to …'

'I know,' he replied.

But his mind was made up and he didn't pause, and in a few moments more he had helped the kid into the harness he had just taken off and was hauling him to his feet, half dragging him to the open hatch.

He lifted Lloyd's hand to the release clip, afraid that in his delirium he might forget.

'When you're clear, pull it,' he said. 'Remember the drill?'

'Thank you,' Lloyd said, turning a final time as he sat on the edge, and lifting his hand to his temple in salute.

Zack answered with a sad and weary half salute of his own.

Then the other man tumbled out into the sky and was gone. Zack knelt by the hatch and watched him fall, saw the chute open far below them, and wondered if he was the only one left on the bomber, or if the pilot had remained to keep them on course until everyone was out. He guessed he'd never know. The ship was disintegrating around him. Every piece of timber seemed to be on fire, and the heat and smoke were overwhelming. His wounded arm throbbed with pain as he slumped at last to the floor and the heat of it burned through his pants, scalding the skin of his thigh beneath it.

As the plane began at last to break apart around him, his last thought before the darkness came to claim him was the prettiness of Peggy's smile, and the fading notes of "As Time Goes By".

Chapter Twenty

1943

Peggy hadn't even known that he was flying that day. It was like that sometimes, he had told her once, a last-minute decision by someone higher up the chain and hardly any time to prepare. So when Freddie first arrived at the pub that night, she had no reason to suspect anything was amiss. But as she made her way across the floor to greet him, she saw the hesitation in his glance, the reluctance in his posture. He had remained by the door, and was turning his forage cap over and over between his fingers.

She swallowed to quell the swelling sense of dread inside her – limbs like liquid, mouth dry – as she crossed the pub towards him. She stopped just before she got to him and when he kept his eyes lowered to the carpet on the ground between them, she had to force her voice to leave her lips.

'Freddie?' His name came out as a whisper, but the evening was quiet and so he heard the word above the soft murmur of conversation. He raised his head.

'What's wrong, Freddie?'

'Can we go somewhere?' He glanced around the pub at the scattered groups of drinkers, and his tone was very even and very calm. 'Somewhere private?'

She nodded, no longer trusting herself to speak, and turned to lead him through to the back of the pub and up the stairs to the sitting room above. She gestured him to one of the armchairs set either side of the low burning fire where the last of the wood was smouldering. The room was warm in its light, and though at another time she would have put another log on, she lacked the will to even think about the possibility. She should offer him tea, she thought, but the impulse receded as soon as it had arisen, and instead she lowered herself on to the chair across from him.

'What's happened?'

Freddie leaned forward, forearms resting on his knees, still twirling the cap between his hands. Peggy watched it spinning, all her attention on the rhythmic movements. It helped to have something to focus on.

'Zack was sent out with another crew this morning, on the *Fine and Dandy*. They ...' He paused and looked up at her at last, waiting until she raised her own head and met his gaze. 'They didn't come back.'

She swallowed. 'Is he dead?' The words seemed to come from someone else's mouth and she flinched at the sound of them.

'I don't know.' Freddie shook his head. 'Some other guys saw parachutes opening, but they couldn't say how many.' He reached for her hands and held them between his own. She could feel the tremor of his muscles, and she realised that though he was trying to be strong for her sake, his own heart was breaking too.

'Oh, Freddie!'

She shifted forward and Freddie folded her into his arms, holding her as she cried, his hands gently stroking her back and shoulders in an automatic gesture of comfort. She kept her face buried against his chest and fought to contain her sobs.

They stayed like that for what seemed a long while until she shifted back and away from him, wiping at her eyes with impatient fingers and blinking to clear away the tears. When she resumed her seat on the armchair, Freddie was gazing into the hearth and watching the pulse and flicker of the embers. His lashes were wet with tears.

Finally, he turned to her again. 'So I guess we just have to wait for news and pray.'

She nodded slowly. She knew it might be months before they heard anything, months of waiting, desperate for news. How could she live with the not-knowing? she wondered. How could she survive?

'If there were parachutes that's hopeful,' Freddie said, and she guessed it was more to reassure himself than to comfort her. 'He may be with the Resistance already, and on his way home.' He gave her a small smile that only served to light her sorrow more brightly.

'Maybe,' she replied, but it was all but impossible to make herself believe it. He shouldn't have been flying that day. He should have been at the base with the others of his crew, standing in the tower and counting the Fortresses in and out, and here now before her alongside his friend.

'Why did he have to go?' she heard herself saying. 'Why him?'

'Wrong place, wrong time.' Freddie shrugged. 'The *Fine and*

Dandy's regular gunner broke his arm yesterday and so they needed a replacement. It just happened to be Zack.'

She said nothing, mind groping for words that would not come, thoughts that refused to cohere into sense. Her eyes searched the rug in front of the hearth as though the answers lay in the threadbare weave.

'I'm so sorry,' Freddie murmured, though she wasn't sure what he was sorry for – he could have done nothing more.

She lifted her head then, touched by his sorrow. 'You don't have to be sorry,' she told him. 'Just promise me you'll tell me the moment you hear anything. The very first moment.'

'Of course.' He nodded.

But she knew even then that it didn't matter – Freddie had already told her all that she needed to know. He had not come home, and some strange sense she could not have explained whispered deep inside her that he never would again. She had lost him, and the sun would never shine as bright again.

'Thank you.'

They sat for a long moment then, neither knowing what else to say. Peggy's gaze swept the pattern of the rug on the floor between them, unseeing. Then, finally bringing the twirling cap to a halt, Freddie got up, and she raised her eyes. He looked so young, but the innocence of his youth was waning fast – she could see the growing sadness in his eyes, and the shadows of his sorrow underneath them.

'I should get back,' he said. 'I'm not supposed to be off base, but I …' He broke off with a shrug.

She stood up too and they stood facing each other in awkward silence before the dying fire. Then, with a nod of farewell, Freddie turned and went to the door. Peggy followed him out into the passage, down the stairs to the pub and out into the high street beyond the door. From there, she watched him disappear along the road towards the airfield as his form was swallowed quickly by the night.

She never saw him again.

Chapter Twenty-One

1943

The war dragged on, seemingly endless, and a war-weary population listened to the reports on the wireless each day without much hope for good news. The Fortresses still thundered over the village every morning, waking Peggy from troubled dreams and rattling the windows in their wake, a brutal reminder of the truth of things.

But even so, each time the pub door opened and she caught a glimpse of uniforms, her heartbeat quickened briefly with a small spark of hope that guttered and died as soon as she saw that Zack was not among them. Mostly now they were strangers, more replacement crews recently arrived from the States.

The weeks passed uncounted, unnoticed, and she worked in the pub in a daze, merely going through the motions of her life, waiting, always waiting for more news that never came.

He was on the run, she told herself a hundred times a day.

He was hiding out with the Resistance and had no way to get word to her.

He would come back to her as soon as the war was over.

Perhaps even sooner.

She had read reports of downed airmen crossing over the Pyrenees into neutral Spain, and in her more hopeful moments she imagined he was on his way back, travelling the long and dangerous road home. But those moments came more rarely with the passing weeks, and that strange sixth sense warned her again and again that he had not been so lucky. At night, when she lay sleepless in the bed they had shared on those stolen nights, she tried sometimes to sense his presence, whispering his name to the silent dark, calling him to her. But not once did she feel so much as a flicker of an answer, and when she drifted into restless fitful sleep at last, her dreams were always full of falling planes and Zack, far away from her and unreachable.

In the midst of her grief and turmoil, almost three months had passed before she realised she was expecting a baby. She had simply failed to notice any of the signs, and when she finally understood what was happening, she really didn't know how to feel about it. The first instinctive flush of excitement was shadowed by sorrow, and any joy at the growing life inside her was tempered by the growing conviction that the child would never know her father. With each new day that brought no news, the slender fragile hope that he might yet be alive diminished a little more, until it was all but impossible to have any faith in his survival at all.

'I think it's just going to be you and me,' she told her child, touching a protective hand to her belly, still in awe that she was going to be a mother. And with a new faith born of desperation, she raised her eyes to the heavens.

'Watch over us, Zack, if you're up there. I'll love you always.'

Despite the season, the morning was cold and bright when she strolled along the high street towards the post office to see her friend and tell her the news. The chilled air was hard in her lungs and the sky a bright clear blue above, the last gasps of winter, reluctant to cede into spring.

Peggy lifted her head to the pale caress of the sun, warmed by the knowledge of the child inside her, and the memory of the light of Zack's love.

In spite of everything, the world was still a beautiful place, and she was glad to be alive.

Chapter Twenty-Two

1995

Georgia walked the short distance to the pub the next morning, still deep in thought, turning over in her mind all that she had read and the final piece of the puzzle that they had talked of late into the night. She could hardly begin to imagine the depth of such a loss, or the pain of so much uncertainty, holding on to a slender thread of hope for two long years that with time and the birth of her child had frayed away into nothing.

Nana had known that the end of the war was the last chance. If Zack had been on the run, hiding out with the Resistance or in a prison camp somewhere, then the end of the war would have brought him back to her at last. But he did not come, and the last dying embers of her hopes flickered and went out completely. By Christmas of 1945, she had steeled herself to a whole life without him, and for her daughter's sake she had needed to look to the future. She couldn't stay at the pub forever – her father's health was beginning to fail, and what would happen to her then? An unmarried mother with no way to support her child. Zack's child. Times were hard for a woman alone, and her choices were few.

So when a nice young engineer she had known before the war moved back to the village and began frequenting the Queen's Head to see her, she allowed herself to be wooed and won, and after weeks of sleepless agonising, Peggy had finally agreed to marry him late in 1946.

She had known from the outset she would never love him. But she liked him – she liked his kindness and generosity, and his unquestioning acceptance of her daughter as his own. The love she had shared with Zack had been the love of a lifetime – precious and rare: she was thankful to have known it even once, and she would call upon the memory of its light to sustain her through all the years she must live without him. Though in the inner sanctum of her thoughts she would never cease to mourn the life that she and Zack had so ardently hoped for, she had been thankful for the chance to start again, knowing there may never be another.

The lunchtime rush at the pub was busier than usual – a rare busload of American tourists all wanting a hurried lunch – and the time flew past in such a flurry of soup and sandwiches and pasties that Georgia barely had time to think. But she was aware of the accents that bounced off the walls, and it was hard not to think of those other Americans who had drunk beneath the pub roof all those years ago, young men like Zack and Freddie, men far from home and at war.

In a brief spare moment she pictured them as her grand-mother had described them – the Americans smart in their uniforms and full of their bravado and the locals seething with resentment. For the first time she could feel their presence, the ghosts of the past reaching out across the years.

It had been a different world, she thought, as she moved to and fro, collecting plates and empties from the bar; how lucky she was to have been born in a time of peace.

At last, the crowd begin to thin and the tourists filed back en masse to the coach that was parked outside. When the last customer had finally stepped through the door, Ben locked it behind them and sat with Georgia at the bar as they took a moment to gather themselves before they set about clearing up the mountains of glasses and dishes, most of them still on the tables waiting to be collected.

'I think we deserve a beer before we clean up,' Ben said, with a smile. 'Would you like one?'

'Yes, please,' she replied.

Though she rarely drank in the daytime it seemed a fitting way to end the shift, and she was grateful for the chance to sit and talk again with Ben a while. He hadn't yet told her the rest of the story he had promised, but she was still hopeful. They had become easy in each other's company, their friendship growing. Clinking their bottles together they drank, and the cool bitter ale was gloriously refreshing.

'Do you think you'll stay on here, in Sutton Heath?' he said, and she looked up sharply in surprise.

'I'm planning to,' she replied. 'I mean, I'm thinking of going to art school but only somewhere local.'

Lately, she had started to make pencil drawings in an old sketch pad she had found in a cupboard, and art school had finally begun to feel like a possibility again.

'But I wasn't thinking of moving away. Why do you ask?'

He lowered his eyes and observed his fingers as they

rubbed at the condensation on the sides of the bottle. She could feel his hesitation, and her heartbeat quickened with nerves for what he might be about to say. Briefly, she wondered if he was going to fire her. After what seemed like a long time, he raised his head and looked at her, his green eyes intent and serious.

'I was wondering if you'd like to have dinner with me one night.'

Her heart seemed to skip a beat. 'I'd love to,' she said, without a moment's pause. 'I really would.'

'It's not too soon after whatshisname?'

She laughed. 'Not at all. I left him, remember? I fell out of love with Scott a long time ago. It just took me a while to realise.'

'That's good. Relationships can be like that sometimes, can't they? You stay because it's easy even if you aren't happy any more.'

She lifted her gaze to meet his, and there was no laughter in his eyes now – she could see the shadow of something painful in their depths, and her heart tightened in her chest with sorrow.

'Is that what happened to you?'

He slid his eyes away from hers and nodded. 'Yes. That's what happened to me. Only I wasn't the one to end it.'

'I'm so sorry,' she whispered. She couldn't think what else to say.

He looked up then and gave her a determined smile.

'It's okay,' he said. 'It was a while ago now, and I'm looking to the future.'

She understood: the hurt was still raw. But he had asked her out for dinner and that was a new beginning, a step forward to the future for them both. She felt the colour rise in her cheeks at the thought of it and took another mouthful of her beer.

'I'm glad you're staying,' he said.

'Me too,' she replied, with a smile. 'I wouldn't want to be anywhere else.'

Then she cast a look once more across the dishes and plates, scattered across the tables.

'Better clear up,' she said, getting to her feet.

'I'll help you,' he answered, and together they set to work again.

Epilogue

1996

Early January, and beyond the kitchen window a low sun burned in a bright cold sky, the branches rimed with frost.

Zack's sister sat at the table with Nana, while Georgia made the tea. Up above, she could hear the tread of footsteps and the rumble of male voices as Ben and Duncan carried the suitcases to the guest bedroom upstairs. But here in the kitchen, the air prickled with awkwardness – in spite of so much love and goodwill between them no one quite knew what to say to get started. Georgia was glad to have something to do.

'Well,' Louise said into the silence at last, her voice soft and low. 'This is harder than I thought it would be.'

She reached for Peggy's hand across the table and the two women smiled at each other. Georgia set down the tea things.

'It's a lovely house,' Louise offered, looking around her. Green eyes, Georgia noticed, with lines at the corners that crinkled when she smiled, and she wondered if Zack's eyes had been the same.

'Thank you,' Nana replied, her voice unsteady with

emotion. Then, 'I'm so happy that you're here at last. All these years ...'

'I know,' Louise replied, her fingers still holding Nana's. 'I know. But we found each other in the end, and that's what counts.'

The silence softened a little. Georgia poured the tea, and a moment later the men appeared in the doorway. Duncan, who was grey and neat with a kind and open face, gave them all a smile.

'It's a beautiful house,' he said.

'I just said the same thing,' Louise laughed.

Ben gestured to Duncan to take a seat, then slid into the chair close beside Georgia, who felt the warmth of his presence as a flush of pleasure inside her. There was another silence but it was more comfortable this time, and they each took sips of their tea.

Louise set down her cup and lifted her handbag to her lap, rummaging inside for a moment before she withdrew a small dark-coloured box, embossed with gold lettering. As she laid it on the table in the space between Nana and herself, Georgia's heart seemed to stop in her chest. She held her breath. Beside her, Ben reached for her fingers and squeezed.

Nana's hand trembled as she reached for it, and no one spoke, the silence bright with meaning.

Slowly, Nana's fingers closed on the little box and she lifted it towards her, hesitantly, as if she couldn't quite believe what she was seeing. Then, with a long outward breath that seemed loud in the hush, she flicked open the lid.

Zack's medal on a pale blue ribbon.

A gold star surrounded by a laurel wreath.

The image of the Statue of Liberty in the centre.

And the word VALOR.

Nana ran her fingers across it, barely brushing the surface, reverent.

'Take it out of the box, why don't you?' Duncan suggested, and Nana's head snapped up, as though surprised to find she was not alone. She shook her head, and turned tear-filled eyes towards Louise.

'It should go to Georgia,' she whispered, and held Louise's gaze as though seeking her agreement.

'I think so too,' the other woman said. 'To his grand-daughter.'

Georgia exchanged a quick glance with Ben, who nodded his encouragement and gave her fingers a final squeeze before letting them go. Then, rising from her chair she went to stand beside her grandmother. Slowly, as though she were suddenly weary, Nana got up from her own seat, and held out the medal for Georgia to take.

For a moment they stood facing each other as though frozen, the medal in its box between them, until finally, Georgia took it in her hands. It was beautiful – gold and green, and still burnished bright as new.

'Thank you,' she whispered, tears too close behind her eyes to say any more. But she drew Nana into a hug and they held each other tightly for a long time.

When they parted, all the awkwardness of before seemed to have completely fallen away. Georgia moved around the table to embrace her great aunt, and the conversation began to flow again with the ease of long friendship and the bonds of family.

Afterword

When the Light Still Shone is fiction. But Zack and Peggy's experiences are based on fact.

During the course of World War II, the Eighth Air Force (the Mighty Eighth) became the largest air force in the world, able to send over 2,000 heavy bombers and over 1,000 fighter planes on a single mission. Such air supremacy paved the way for the D-Day invasion. By May 1945, the young men of the Eighth had flown more than 6,000 sorties and dropped 670,000 tons of bombs.

But the cost was enormous.

26,000 Eighth Air Force airmen were killed in action.

28,000 became prisoners of war.

For their bravery they were awarded 17 Medals of Honor, 220 Distinguished Service Crosses and over 420,000 Air Medals.

You can read more about the Mighty Eighth at
https://www.mightyeighth.org

Also by Samantha Grosser

ECHOES OF WAR

Welcome to the *Echoes of War* series. Set in Britain in the shadow of World War II, these gripping standalone historical novels of love, loss, and courage will stay with you long after turning the final page.

Available from all good online bookstores.

Another Time and Place - Preview

He wasn't coming back.

She waited for him at the hotel near the air base, roused from dreams by the sortie of bombers flying east overhead, lying shattered and sweating, awake but still in the nightmare.

Dragging herself from the warmth of the bed, she shivered as the winter air touched bare skin, and dressed hurriedly in the semi-darkness of the morning. Downstairs, the hotel was just beginning to stir and outside, shadows made their way here and there across the village.

She walked all morning to fill the space before the bombers returned, unable to find peace, her steps always drawn towards the air base, waiting, waiting. She bought a *Daily Express* from the shop in the village and saw the words Monte Cassino in the headline, but the name held no meaning for her and she tossed the paper aside on the hotel bed, unopened.

It was lunchtime when the planes returned, a distant drone that rose to the familiar roar, and she raced down three flights of stairs to stand on the street, watching the damaged aircraft flying low across the village, searching among them for the *American Maiden*, unable to make out the names. She almost ran to the base as the planes came into land one after another, and the silence of the afternoon was deafening when the last engine finally died. Pacing back and forth, never far from the gate, she waited till the chill of the evening began to settle around her and the light to leave the sky, before she returned to the hotel, arms wrapped around herself against the cold, useless because the cold was inside her.

She waited all night for him, refusing to believe that he hadn't returned, wrapped in her arms, cold and in pain, hating each footstep on the stairs that wasn't his. Staring into the fire, she hoped against hope that there was some other explanation, that some miracle might bring him to her even now. But the morning light brought no relief, just the thunder of another mission flying overhead and the growing realisation of the truth. He wasn't coming back.

But she waited still, unable to leave, walking again in the lanes near the base as though by being close to where he should be he would come. Once, she approached the gate, wanting to ask the sentry, desperate for information, but at the last moment she backed away, knowing he would tell her nothing, that she had no proof of who she was.

Late in the afternoon, as the winter light ceded easily to the darkness, she retraced her steps to the hotel and another night of fitful sleeping, dreams of fire and falling planes. Then finally, as the sun rose once more behind its shroud of grey, she understood that he would not come, so she packed her few belongings, paid the bill with the money he had given her, and went outside to wait for the bus that would take her home.

Another Time and Place

is available from all good online bookstores.

Rations and Recipes: a Brief Journey Back to the Cookery of World War II

Go to www.samgrosserbooks.com
to get your FREE copy of Recipes from World War II.

About the Author

Historical fiction author Samantha Grosser has an Honours Degree in English Literature and spent many years teaching English both in Asia and Australia. Although she originally hails from England, she now lives in Sydney, Australia, with her husband and son.

You can sign up for news and special offers at her website: samgrosserbooks.com

 facebook.com/samgrosserbooks
 instagram.com/samgrosserbooks
 goodreads.com/Samantha_Grosser

Made in the USA
Middletown, DE
15 November 2024